# The Yellow House Mystery

*The Boxcar Children Mysteries*

The Boxcar Children
Surprise Island
The Yellow House Mystery
Mystery Ranch
Mike's Mystery
Blue Bay Mystery
The Woodshed Mystery
The Lighthouse Mystery
Mountain Top Mystery
Schoolhouse Mystery
Caboose Mystery
Houseboat Mystery
Snowbound Mystery
Tree House Mystery
Bicycle Mystery
Mystery in the Sand
Mystery Behind the Wall
Bus Station Mystery
Benny Uncovers a Mystery
The Haunted Cabin Mystery
The Deserted Library Mystery
The Animal Shelter Mystery
The Old Motel Mystery
The Mystery of the Hidden Painting
The Amusement Park Mystery
The Mystery of the Mixed-Up Zoo
The Camp-Out Mystery
The Mystery Girl
The Mystery Cruise
The Disappearing Friend Mystery
The Mystery of the Singing Ghost
Mystery in the Snow
The Pizza Mystery
The Mystery Horse
The Mystery at the Dog Show
The Castle Mystery
The Mystery of the Lost Village
The Mystery on the Ice
The Mystery of the Purple Pool
The Ghost Ship Mystery
The Mystery in Washington, DC
The Canoe Trip Mystery
The Mystery of the Hidden Beach
The Mystery of the Missing Cat
The Mystery at Snowflake Inn
The Mystery on Stage
The Dinosaur Mystery
The Mystery of the Stolen Music
The Mystery at the Ball Park
The Chocolate Sundae Mystery
The Mystery of the Hot Air Balloon
The Mystery Bookstore
The Pilgrim Village Mystery
The Mystery of the Stolen Boxcar
The Mystery in the Cave
The Mystery on the Train
The Mystery at the Fair
The Mystery of the Lost Mine
The Guide Dog Mystery
The Hurricane Mystery
The Pet Shop Mystery
The Mystery of the Secret Message
The Firehouse Mystery
The Mystery in San Francisco
The Niagara Falls Mystery
The Mystery at the Alamo
The Outer Space Mystery
The Soccer Mystery
The Mystery in the Old Attic
The Growling Bear Mystery
The Mystery of the Lake Monster
The Mystery at Peacock Hall
The Windy City Mystery
The Black Pearl Mystery
The Cereal Box Mystery
The Panther Mystery
The Mystery of the Queen's Jewels
The Stolen Sword Mystery
The Basketball Mystery

The Movie Star Mystery
The Mystery of the Pirate's Map
The Ghost Town Mystery
The Mystery of the Black Raven
The Mystery in the Mall
The Mystery in New York
The Gymnastics Mystery
The Poison Frog Mystery
The Mystery of the Empty Safe
The Home Run Mystery
The Great Bicycle Race Mystery
The Mystery of the Wild Ponies
The Mystery in the Computer Game
The Mystery at the Crooked House
The Hockey Mystery
The Mystery of the Midnight Dog
The Mystery of the Screech Owl
The Summer Camp Mystery
The Copycat Mystery
The Haunted Clock Tower Mystery
The Mystery of the Tiger's Eye
The Disappearing Staircase Mystery
The Mystery on Blizzard Mountain
The Mystery of the Spider's Clue
The Candy Factory Mystery
The Mystery of the Mummy's Curse
The Mystery of the Star Ruby
The Stuffed Bear Mystery
The Mystery of Alligator Swamp
The Mystery at Skeleton Point
The Tattletale Mystery
The Comic Book Mystery
The Great Shark Mystery
The Ice Cream Mystery
The Midnight Mystery
The Mystery in the Fortune Cookie
The Black Widow Spider Mystery
The Radio Mystery
The Mystery of the Runaway Ghost
The Finders Keepers Mystery
The Mystery of the Haunted Boxcar
The Clue in the Corn Maze
The Ghost of the Chattering Bones
The Sword of the Silver Knight
The Game Store Mystery
The Mystery of the Orphan Train
The Vanishing Passenger
The Giant Yo-Yo Mystery
The Creature in Ogopogo Lake
The Rock 'n' Roll Mystery
The Secret of the Mask
The Seattle Puzzle
The Ghost in the First Row
The Box That Watch Found
A Horse Named Dragon
The Great Detective Race
The Ghost at the Drive-In Movie
The Mystery of The Traveling Tomatoes

# The Yellow

# House Mystery

*by*

**Gertrude Chandler Warner**

*Illustrated by*

Mary Gehr

ALBERT WHITMAN & COMPANY
Morton Grove, Illinois

978-0-8075-9365-3 (hardcover)
978-0-8075-9366-0 (paperback)



110 LB 14 13 12 11 10

Printed in the U.S.A.

# Contents

CHAPTER 1

# The Cave

Four lively children lived with their grandfather Alden in a big house. The children's father and mother had died years before. Their cousin Joe lived in the big house too. He was grown up and his cousins thought he was great fun.

First there was Henry Alden, who was sixteen and in high school. Jessie Alden came next. She was in high school too. Violet was a pretty dark-haired little girl of twelve, and Benny was seven.

Benny was on his way home from school one day in Spring. The minute he went into the house, he heard the telephone ringing. Then he heard Mrs. McGregor, the housekeeper, answering it.

"It's for you, Benny," she said. She was excited. "It's your cousin Joe."

Benny went to the telephone. "Hello, Joe," he said.

"We're going to blast, Benny!" Joe called over the telephone. "The men are almost ready to blast the top off the cave. They say that you children can come over to the island, if you stay right with me. You get the others and come along over."

"O.K. Joe!" cried Benny. "We'll come just as quickly as we can." He hurried to the hall to tell his brother Henry. For this cave was one the children had found themselves the summer before. They had crawled in to see how far they could go. Without trying, they had found some Indian tools in the sand which Joe said were very wonderful.

Now, their grandfather had sent some men to the island to take the top off the cave, so that it would be easier to dig the things out.

"Was that Joe? What did he want?" asked Henry. He came out into the hall.

"He said the men are going to blast the cave open!" shouted Benny. "Last summer he told us we couldn't come that day, and now he says we can."

Benny ran upstairs two steps at a time, calling, 'Jess! Jess! Vi! Vi!"

"Well, what's the matter now, Benny?" asked Jessie, looking up from her school work.

"The men are going to blast the cave on Surprise Island, and we have to hurry and go over."

"Who said so?" asked Jessie.

"Joe," answered Benny. "He just telephoned to me."

"But we can't go without Grandfather," said Violet, softly.

"Grandfather is just driving into the yard," Henry called loudly up the stairs. "Hurry and come down before he puts the car away!"

Mr. Alden could not understand a word at first, because everyone talked at once. But his driver seemed to be turning the car around anyway. Mr. Alden was smiling to himself about something.

"Did Joe call you, too, Grandfather?" cried Henry.

Mr. Alden laughed. "Well—" he said, "we'll go down to the dock and over to the island in the motorboat."

"I hope Captain Daniel will have the boat on

this side," said Henry. "Joe seems to be in a hurry, and the men won't wait for us for very long."

"Oh, I hope they won't blast until we get there," cried Benny.

"I don't think they will," said Mr. Alden smiling. "If Joe sent for you, he will wait until you have time to get there."

"Of course he will, Grandfather," said Jessie. "There is Captain Daniel on the dock already."

It was true. Captain Daniel smiled when he saw the four children coming with their grandfather. He liked them all.

"I'm waiting," he said, "and Joe is waiting on the island and so are the workmen. Joe said they won't blast until you are all there."

"Good. I'm glad," said Benny, getting into the boat and sitting down.

They were soon on their way across the water to the island where they had spent such a happy summer the year before. They were all thinking of that exciting day when they had found the cave.

Benny looked at the captain. "I don't suppose you remember the Indian things we found in that cave, Captain?" he said.

"Indeed I do," said the captain with a laugh. "You children didn't know then that Mr. Joe dug up things for a living. But I did. I knew Mr. Joe when he was a little boy."

"Remember how excited Joe was?" cried Jessie. "He wouldn't even let us dig any more inside the cave."

"That was all right though, Jessie," said Henry. "He wanted things done right. These workmen know how to dig better than we do."

"And here we are, going to blast the top off the cave!" said Benny.

"There's Joe now," said Jessie. "Who in the world is that with him? It's a girl!"

"That's not a girl," said Benny. "That's a lady."

"Well, anyway, she isn't very old," said Jessie.

"She's awfully pretty," said Benny, as they came nearer.

"Hello, children," cried Joe, as the boat stopped at the dock. "This is Alice Wells. She came over to look at the Indian things you found. She knows lots about such things."

"That must be interesting work," said Jessie to Alice, shaking hands. She liked Alice at once. She had such a beautiful smile.

"Yes, it is," said Alice. "I feel as if I knew every one of you. This is Benny, I'm sure. And Violet. And Henry. Joe has told me so much about you all." She smiled at Mr. Alden as if she already knew him well.

Benny took Alice's hand. "Let's go right off and see them blast," he said.

"This is going to be fun for you, Benny," said Mr. Alden, smiling at the little boy. "The men are going to let you push the handle to set off the blast."

"Oh boy," cried Benny. "Where is the handle?"

Joe led the way without a word. Past the little yellow house, past the barn where they had lived the summer before, past the beach. There beside a crowd of workmen, they saw a handle in the ground.

"Here they are," said one of the workmen. "Are you the little boy who is going to set off this blast? Now, you take hold of that handle and push it down as far as you can."

Benny did as he was told. From far away down the island came a loud noise like thunder. Then the children saw a great cloud of smoke, and then flying rocks.

"What a noise that was!" cried Benny. They all watched the smoke still coming from the cave.

"Very good," said Joe. "Let's go."

Down the path they went. Soon they came to the cave. The big rocks were broken into small pieces, and the men started to take them away. The whole cave was open. The children watched quietly.

"I suppose nobody can dig in the cave until all those rocks are lifted off," said Henry at last.

"That's right," said Joe. "They will be taking rocks off for days. Really there is nothing more to see now."

"You mean we'd better go home then?" said Mr. Alden. He winked at Benny.

"Well, I don't care too much," said Benny. "Anyway, we blasted and that's more than I expected."

"You will come over many times when we get to digging," said Alice. "We have already taken away the shell pile and all the things in it."

"The Museum people were delighted with all the things," said Joe. "You found some things that they had never seen before."

"That's right," said Alice. "Joe and I are going to try to find out what they all are. I shall be working on them for a year maybe, and maybe longer."

"That's good," said Benny. "You come up to our house and see us." He was surprised when Joe laughed.

At supper that same night, Benny sat thinking.

"What's the matter, Ben?" asked Henry kindly. "Aren't you going to eat your supper?"

"Oh, yes," said Benny looking up. "I was just thinking."

"What about?" Violet asked gently.

"Well," replied Benny slowly, "I was thinking about Alice. I think Joe likes her. I think that's why he wanted us to go home."

"Well," laughed Jessie, "what of it? Didn't you like her yourself?"

"Oh, yes," cried Benny. "I liked her a lot. But that's different. I think Joe is going to marry her."

"What!" shouted Henry. "How can you tell? Joe just met her today."

"Oh, no, he didn't, my boy," said Mr. Alden. "Joe and Alice went to school together when they were children. Alice has been away a long time. She just came back to do this work for Joe."

"Well, I wish Joe *would* get married," said Jessie. "It must be lonesome for him living all alone on the top floor of this house with a lot of children like us."

"And an old man like me!" said her grandfather. "But I'll tell you something. I watched Joe and Alice today and I think Benny is right.

But don't say a word. Let's wait and see what happens."

"Yes, let's," said Benny. "But you'll see they will get married all right." Then he started to eat his supper.

CHAPTER 2

# A Wedding

What a day it was for the Alden children when the rocks were all taken away. The floor of the cave was smooth sand, just right for digging. More men came to the island that day, and the digging began.

"Isn't it funny to see grown-up men digging in the sand," said Benny.

"Watch them, Benny," said Alice. "You will see them put things in that big box."

Sure enough, the men often found broken

pieces of a dish, or a smooth stone, and carefully put them in a box. The children never grew tired of watching them. Every day after school they went over to the island to see what the men had found.

Henry could not come until late on some days, for he had to row with the high school crew on the river. He had been Captain of the high school crew for a year. But as soon as he came, he always helped Joe carry the boxes to the boat.

One day the box was so heavy that Henry

could not get it to the boat. "I'm sorry, Joe," he said. "Let's stop here at the yellow house and sit down for a minute. This is harder work than rowing."

Joe was glad too, to sit down on the wooden steps of the little yellow house.

Soon Benny was looking in all the windows. "Let's go into this house some time," he said.

"I wonder why we never did, Joe," said Jessie. "Do you know why Grandfather doesn't like to talk about it?"

"No," said Joe. "I never asked him because he seemed so sad about it. I think it has a mystery. Some day Alice and I are going into the house and solve the mystery."

"Without us?" cried Benny.

"Yes, sir, without anybody!" said Joe.

"You don't *really* mean you'd go without us?" Benny asked. He could hardly believe his ears.

"Don't tease him, Joe," said Alice suddenly. She put her hand gently on Joe's arm. "Let's tell him! Let's tell them all!"

"Ho-hum. Maybe you don't need to tell us. Maybe we can guess," cried Benny.

"All right. Go ahead and guess," laughed Joe. He took Alice's hand and held it.

"You make it too easy," said Benny. He looked at Henry. "Didn't I tell you? I told you a long time ago."

"It wasn't true a long time ago," said Joe.

"Let's guess," said Violet, taking Alice's other hand. "Does the secret have anything to do with music?"

"Yes!" said Joe and Benny together.

"Will everyone wear beautiful clothes?" asked Jessie smiling.

"Yes," answered Joe and Benny.

"Will there be a cake, and maybe a beautiful ring?" asked Henry.

"Right here!" said Joe. He held up Alice's hand. On it was a beautiful new ring.

"Funny we didn't see that," said Jessie.

"Not so funny, dear," said Alice. "It went on just this minute."

"For good," said Joe.

"Where are you going to live, Alice?" Violet asked suddenly.

"Well, you know Joe has the whole top floor of that big house all to himself," Alice said. "He says he needs company, so we will live there together."

"Oh, boy! Right in the same house with us, just the same as ever!" Benny shouted.

"Does Grandfather know?" asked Henry.

"Well, yes," said Joe. "We told him yesterday. He said we could have the top floor. After all, it's his house."

"Will the wedding be in our house too?" asked Jessie.

"Yes. We want Violet to play the wedding music on her violin, and we want Watch to wear a big white ribbon and come to the wedding too."

"He won't like the ribbon," said Benny. "But he won't bark if Jessie tells him not to. When is the wedding going to be?"

"As soon as you get out of school," answered Joe. "Then, you children won't be busy. And

Alice and I will have done a lot of work in the cave."

"I can't wait till school is out," said Benny.

"I guess you'll have to," laughed Joe.

What a wedding the Alden wedding was! Everyone talked about it afterward for days. Alice was very lovely in her beautiful white dress. Violet played for the wedding on her violin, with three other players. She wore a long violet dress. Jessie wore blue.

Watch wore his big white ribbon, and he did not bark until it was all over. When everyone was out on the porch saying good-by to Joe and Alice, he barked and barked. By then it didn't matter, for everyone was laughing and talking.

The children did not know what to do with themselves right after Joe and Alice had gone. They tried to read. When it was almost time for supper, Jessie said, "I wonder where they are going on their wedding trip."

"I don't know myself," said her grandfather. "People don't tell where they are going."

"They will be back in two weeks," said Violet. "Let's go upstairs again and look at their lovely home."

Even Mr. Alden went up with the children. Watch came along too. He was always happy when he was with his four children.

Mr. Alden sat down in a big easy chair while Violet and Jessie looked again at the pretty blue and white kitchen. They went into the sunny bedroom, and back to the pleasant living room.

The new dishes were set in piles in the clean cupboards. "It will be such fun for them to keep house here," cried Jessie. "Everything is in such good order. Alice will love it."

"Won't we have a wonderful time this summer," said Benny. "When Joe comes back he is sure to have some fine ideas."

"Maybe they won't want us around, though," said Jessie. "We must be careful about that."

"Well then," said Benny, "*we* can think up the ideas, and ask them to do things with us."

"A very good plan, my boy," said Mr. Alden with a smile. "If they don't want to, they can always say no."

Then they heard a step on the stairs. It was Mrs. McGregor, the housekeeper. She was a kind little lady, and took fine care of the children. Her hair was white and her eyes were blue.

"Supper is ready," she said with a smile.

"I hope I can have some more wedding cake," said Benny. "I just love weddings, don't you, Mrs. McGregor?" He took her hand.

"Yes, my dear," said Mrs. McGregor, smiling at the little boy. "Your cousin Joe has a fine wife, and he is a fine young man himself. It was a lovely wedding."

Then Violet thought, as she had often thought before, that there was something sad about Mrs. McGregor. "Yes," she said to herself, "she is sad even when she smiles."

CHAPTER 3

# The Mystery

The children were lonesome after the wedding. They longed so much for Joe and Alice. But just then the mystery of the little yellow house began.

Supper was over. Warm air was blowing through the open windows, and birds were singing their evening songs.

As Mr. Alden sat down in his easy chair, he said with a pleasant smile, "Isn't it time to think about summer plans?"

Henry looked at his grandfather.

"Grandfather," he said, "do you mind if I ask you something?"

"No, of course not," said Mr. Alden. "Ask anything you like."

"You may not think it is polite," said Henry slowly.

"But what is a grandfather for?" asked Mr. Alden, winking at Benny. "I know you are very polite to me always. Go ahead and don't be afraid."

"Well," said Henry, "do you remember last fall I asked you why we never went into the little yellow house on Surprise Island? You looked very cross for a minute, and Jessie and I were sure we had hurt your feelings."

Jessie went on, "Don't you remember? You said, 'That's another story.' "

"Oh, I remember all right," said Mr. Alden. "I never could forget that." He looked from one face to another. "If you four children will come over here and sit down on the floor, I'll tell you all about it. I guess the time has come when you ought to know."

Mr. Alden waited until they were ready to listen, and then he began.

"You know I told you my father built the barn on Surprise Island for his best race horses? And that the man who took care of the horses built the little yellow house for himself?

"The man's name was Bill. He was about thirty years old then and so was I. I loved Bill very much. He took fine care of the race horses, and he lived in the little yellow house with his good wife."

"Race horses!" cried Benny. "Did they race?"

"Yes, they raced while my father was living. My father was your great-grandfather, you know. Bill loved the horses, and he was a good, kind man. But I must tell you he was weak."

"Not very strong, you mean?" said Benny.

"No, Benny," said Mr. Alden sadly. "I don't mean that at all. He was a very strong man. He could lift the boat. I mean he had a weak will. Anybody could tell him what to do." Mr. Alden stopped.

"Don't tell us, if you don't want to!" begged Jessie.

"Yes, I want to tell you now. I'm afraid Bill was a coward. He would do anything his brother Sam told him. His brother had some bad friends."

The children were suddenly very quiet. They knew that this was a sad story for their grandfather to tell.

"Let me go and get Watch, please!" cried Benny. "I'll be right back."

Everyone had to smile as Benny disappeared into the kitchen. They knew that Benny always wanted the dog when things did not go just right. He came back at once with Watch running after him.

"Lie down, old fellow," said Henry. Watch lay down beside Benny and put his head on his paws.

"Well, one evening," Mr. Alden went on, "Bill's wife, Margaret, noticed that Bill seemed to have something on his mind. He would not talk about it. After she had gone to bed, she heard a queer grating noise in the front room where Bill was. She got up and went to see what he was doing.

"There he sat. reading the paper. The noise had stopped. He asked her what she wanted and she told him about the queer noise. He said it must have been the waves on the rocks.

"But it wasn't waves, and Margaret knew it. She began to be very much worried. She went back to bed and pretended to be asleep, and the noise began again."

"Didn't she ever find out what it was?" asked Benny.

"No, Benny, she never did. To this day, nobody knows what Bill was doing in that front room. This went on for two nights. The next night Margaret smelled something queer. She thought it might be paint. But when she came out, Bill was not painting. He was reading."

"Then one night he went out to the barn to see the horses, and he never came back."

"*Never* came back?" asked Violet.

"No. Margaret waited an hour. Then she took a light and went out to look for him. He had given the horses water, but he had left the barn door open. The rowboat was gone. Then Margaret telephoned to me. I got up and dressed and found a policeman. Captain Daniel took us over to the island in another boat. But of course it was dark and we couldn't find a thing."

"No clues?" said Benny.

"That's right—no clues," said Mr. Alden. "Next day the island was full of policemen. They looked under the barn, under the dock, all through the woods. But they couldn't find Bill. They found Bill's rowboat a few days later. It was tied up at another dock about a mile away on the mainland."

"Did they radio the news?" asked Benny. "And get the F.B.I. men?"

"Oh, *think*, Benny!" said Henry. "There weren't any radios then."

"Oh, I forgot that," said Benny. "But at last they found him, didn't they?"

"No, they never found Bill." Mr. Alden stopped and then went on again.

"Margaret thought the clues were the queer smell and the grating noise in the front room. So the police went all over the little yellow house. They thought they might find a letter. Margaret thought she had seen Bill reading one."

"You mean maybe a letter frightened Bill?" said Henry.

"Yes, that's right. But they never found one. They took up the rugs. They hunted all through the desk. They even went down the chimney with a light."

"Did they take up the floor boards?" asked Henry.

"No, they didn't take them up. But they looked at every board in the house. There was dust between every two boards."

"Why didn't they put a notice in the newspapers?" asked Violet.

"They did. We had a notice in the paper every day for two years. But nothing ever came of it."

"I'm so sorry for Margaret," said Violet. "She must be old now."

"Yes, my dear," said her grandfather with a smile. "She seems old to you, I know."

"*Seems* old?" said Violet. "Do I know her?"

"Yes, you all know her very well," said Mr. Alden. "She is Mrs. McGregor."

"Mrs. McGregor!" shouted all the children. They could not believe it. For Mrs. McGregor had taken care of them, and listened to their troubles ever since they had come to live with their grandfather. They could not think of her as young, or as anyone in a mystery.

At last Henry said, "I suppose she couldn't live alone on the island, and so Great-grandfather gave her a home here?"

"That's right. He asked her to come here to live with us as our housekeeper, and the next year he died. She has lived here ever since. We never talk about Bill now, and nobody has ever been inside the yellow house since that time."

"It's such a lovely little house!" cried Jessie. "It's too bad it's such a sad place and nobody can live there."

Henry sat up and put his hand on his grandfather's knee.

"Grandfather!" he said, "couldn't *we* go into the little yellow house? I do wish you'd let us. Just let us look around. We might find something."

Mr. Alden looked at Henry and smiled. "You're a good boy, Henry. But do you really think you could find anything when the police couldn't?"

"No, I suppose not," said Henry.

But just the same, all the children kept looking at their grandfather.

Suddenly he leaned forward. "Do you really want to go?" he asked.

"Oh, yes!" they all answered.

"Well, all right. You may go. You may hunt around all you like, and see what you can find."

Then Benny said, "I don't want to go."

"You don't want to *go!*" shouted Henry. "Why not?"

"Well, I think it would be mean to go without Joe and Alice," said Benny. "They won't come home from their wedding trip for two weeks."

"Is *that* all?" cried Jessie. "You scared me, Benny. I thought you really didn't want to go."

"We'd all like to wait," said Violet. "It will be much more fun if Joe and Alice go with us."

"Wouldn't it be wonderful if we found something? Some clue?" cried Henry.

"Yes, it would," said Mr. Alden. "But I don't think you will. Don't talk about this to Mrs. McGregor yet, will you?"

"We won't," promised Henry. "Look, Benny, you won't tell, will you?"

"I never tell secrets, do I?" asked Benny. "I never told where Joe and Alice went on their wedding trip, did I?"

"Do you *know?*" asked Henry, in great surprise.

"Of course I do."

"You do?" said Mr. Alden. "I don't know myself. Nobody told *me*."

"They told me I could tell you two days after the wedding. That's right now."

"Well, where did they go?" cried Jessie.

"They went to our barn on Surprise Island," said Benny. "That was another surprise, because they are so near, and everyone thinks they are far away."

"Just think of that! Our very own barn where we stayed last summer!" cried Jessie.

"That's right," said Benny. He was delighted to surprise even his grandfather.

"Well," said Henry, "now I can hardly wait for them to come home."

"I shan't sleep a wink tonight," said Jessie. "I shall be thinking of Joe and Alice, and the little yellow house."

They all expected to stay awake all night, but they were soon all sleeping quietly, even Watch.

CHAPTER 4

# The Tin Box

It seemed a long time to the four children before Joe and Alice came home. But at last they drove up to the front door in a new station wagon.

"It's Joe!" shouted Benny. "He's got a new station wagon!" He ran down the steps. "Oh, Joe, why did you buy a station wagon when there are only two of you?"

"Guess!" said Joe, laughing. He jumped out and gave his hand to his beautiful young wife.

Then the other children ran out to see Joe and Alice. Everyone was laughing and talking at once. They took bags and boxes and went into the house. Watch barked and jumped around, to show how glad he was to see Joe again.

"I bet you got a station wagon so we could go too," cried Benny.

"That's right," said Alice, smiling at him. "Won't we have a lot of fun in that station wagon!"

"We know where to go first," Benny went on. "Want us to tell you?"

"Children, children! Do let Alice sit down one minute," said Mr. Alden as he came out into the hall. "You have lots of time, you know. Come in, Alice, and let them talk."

But the children could not wait. Before they knew it, they were telling all about the mystery of the little yellow house.

"What a story!" said Joe. "I've wondered about that house myself. I'd like to go inside."

"We waited for you to go with us," said Henry.

"Will you both go?" asked Jessie.

"Of course we will," said Alice.

Joe laughed. "Well," he said, "it looks as if we would go right back to Surprise Island."

"Today?" cried Benny.

"Yes, today!" said Joe and Alice together.

Mr. Alden laughed. "Let's have lunch first," he said.

"You're right, Grandfather," said Violet. "Alice ought to see the presents in her house. Beautiful dishes and things. They came after the wedding, Alice."

"Lots of food, too," said Benny. "All in tin cans. A whole ham. And whole chickens and things. But won't you eat lunch with us just to-day?"

"Of course we will," said Joe. "You can show us the tin cans when we come back from the island. How will that be?"

"Fine," said Benny. "We can go to the dock in the new station wagon. I guess Captain Daniel will be surprised to see us."

"I guess so, too," laughed Joe. "We just said good-by to him."

Soon it was time for lunch. Henry was thinking what to take to the yellow house. "I shall take my tools," he said to Jessie, as he sat beside her at the table. "Maybe we'll need them. I don't think of anything else, do you?"

"A flashlight," said Joe, who had heard them. "There aren't any lights there."

"Oh, thank you, Joe," cried Jessie. "I'm glad you don't think we are silly to go."

"Indeed I don't. It sounds very interesting. Alice thinks so, too."

"You did pick out a very nice girl," said Benny.

"Thank you, Benny," said Alice laughing.

"Is there room for me?" asked Mr. Alden, to everyone's surprise.

"Room for you!" said Violet going over to her grandfather. "There's always room for you!"

Just the same, they were all surprised and delighted that Mr. Alden wanted to go.

"There are chairs for you to sit in," said Benny. "I saw them through the window. Oh, I wish we were there this minute."

In about an hour, Benny had his wish. The

whole family left the boat at the dock on Surprise Island, and now stood at the front steps of the little yellow house. They went up the four wooden steps. Mr. Alden himself opened the door. They went in the front room and looked around.

There was a table in the middle of the room. Old papers were on it. There was a fireplace with a brick chimney painted white on one side of the room. There was a desk on the other side. Everything was covered with dust.

"This is the very room where Bill sat reading the paper, Joe," said Henry.

"The queer grating noise came from this room," said Jessie.

"Now," began Henry, "let's look around and see what *could* make a grating noise."

"The drawer in the table," said Alice.

"The drawers in the desk," said Mr. Alden.

"The boards in the floor," said Jessie.

"The chimney," said Benny.

Everyone looked at the strong brick chimney and smiled at the little boy. But Henry said kindly, "That's right, Benny."

"We'll look at every brick," said Benny.

"Yes, *you* look at every brick," said Jessie. "You remember the police looked down the chimney with a light, Benny?"

"Yes, I remember, but they looked at the floor boards too, and all the other things you said."

"That's right, too," said Joe. "Now, what's first?"

"The table drawer," said Henry, pulling it out. "Not much here."

"It grates when you pull it," said Alice.

There were two pens in the drawer, two fish hooks, and an old paintbrush.

"The paint!" shouted Henry.

"I don't think this is paint, though," said Joe. He smelled of the paintbrush. "I think this is whitewash."

Everyone was excited. "Maybe we'll find something new, after all, Grandfather," said Jessie. "Did the police know this was whitewash?"

"No, I don't think so," replied Mr. Alden. "They would have taken the paintbrush with them if they had thought it was a clue. The police did not work as well in those days as they do now. You can take the drawer to pieces if you want. Something may be hidden in the cracks."

Henry tapped the drawer with his hammer, and soon took off the sides. But there was nothing there.

"The desk next," said Mr. Alden. "Two drawers in that."

"Maybe a secret drawer," said Joe.

They took out both drawers and put them on the table. "A pen. Some old writing paper. That's all," said Henry.

"Now, look at the floor boards," said Jessie. "We can take up the rugs."

There were two small rugs. Joe looked at them carefully. Then he rolled them up and put them on a chair. The whole family went to work. Mr. Alden sat and watched. Each one took a stick and looked in every crack. Up and down the room they went on their hands and knees.

At last Joe said, "All done. I don't think these floor boards have been moved. I don't think the clue is there."

"Well, then, my chimney!" shouted Benny. "Every, every brick!"

"That will take many days," said Henry laughing. "First we'll tap every brick. You all listen and see if any brick sounds different from the others."

"Let me tap," said Benny. "I thought of the chimney."

"Well," said Joe, "let him tap, Henry. Let me show you, Ben. Tap like this." Joe struck a brick lightly once or twice.

Benny got down on the floor. He started with the first brick. "Tap. Tap. Tap-tap," went his hammer. Then he took the next brick. He tapped just the way Joe had shown him. At last the family sat down, smiling. There were so many bricks.

Suddenly Jessie jumped up. "I think that one sounds different!" she said. She got down beside Benny.

"I don't," said Henry. "Tap it again, Benny."

"Tap. Tap. Tap-tap," went the hammer.

"Well, maybe not," said Jessie. "I thought it did the first time."

In a few minutes Violet said, "Listen again to that one! That one sounds different to me."

"It's right over the first one, Violet," said Benny. "Right over the one Jessie heard."

But it did not sound different to anyone else.

"Go on, my boy," said Mr. Alden leaning forward. "Keep on tapping."

The children all looked up at their grandfather. They were surprised to see that he was excited and very white.

Benny began on another row of bricks. Then it was Mr. Alden himself who said, "Stop there! Tap again!"

"That last one *is* different," cried Joe. "Give me the hammer a minute, Ben!"

But Joe did not use the hammer. He just looked at the brick.

Benny was looking at it too. "Whitewash!" he whispered.

"Whitewash," said Joe. "I do believe that this brick has been taken out and put back again."

"Can you take it out, Joe?" Alice asked excitedly.

"I'm going to try," answered Joe. "We don't want the whole chimney to come down."

"Here's the screwdriver," said Benny.

"Just what I want," cried Joe. "Yes, this brick has certainly been taken out!" He put the screwdriver at the edge of the brick and tapped it with the hammer. Out came dried whitewash.

"What did I tell you?" cried Benny. "New whitewash. Not like the old."

More dried whitewash fell out with every tap of the hammer. "This has certainly been painted to look like the other bricks," said Joe. "But the whitewash is different."

"Now pull it out, Joe!" shouted Benny.

Joe took hold of the brick and pulled. It made a queer grating noise, as he worked it out. At last it came out and fell on the floor.

"Look in the hole! Look in the hole!" yelled Benny. "There's a letter in the hole."

Joe could hardly believe what he saw. But there was the letter. He took it out and read it.

"What in the world does this mean, Uncle James?" he asked, as he handed it to Mr. Alden.

"Read it aloud!" cried the children.

Mr. Alden read:

> *Dear Bill,*
>
> *Thanks for the money. I can make it three times as much if you will help me. Some friends of mine know how. Meet me at your little house in Maine. (Bear Trail) Then you can pay Mr. A. and get your part of the rest* sure. *Look in the tin box. Hide this.*
>
> *S.M.*

"Well, my dears," said Mr. Alden, "now we have a real mystery."

Jessie said, "And we don't know any more than we did."

"Bear Trail," said Benny. "I wonder where that is."

CHAPTER 5

# The Next Move

Mr. Alden read the letter again. Then he said, "Jessie, you say we don't know any more than we did. But I think we do."

"Right," said Jessie, laughing. "I think so myself, now. We know there is something up in Maine anyway."

"Yes, and we know more than that," said her grandfather. "I had better tell you one other thing. Just before Bill disappeared, he sold two fine race horses for your great-grandfather. But he never paid over the money. He kept saying he would, but he never did. I always thought his brother got it away from him, and Bill went away to get it back. I may be wrong."

Joe said, "Maybe Bill was afraid to come back without the money."

"That's what we thought," said Mr. Alden. "You see, the week after Bill disappeared, his brother Sam was killed by a car. So he couldn't help us find Bill."

"Did Mrs. McGregor know about the race horses and the money?" asked Jessie.

"Yes. Poor Margaret! She never got over it," answered Mr. Alden. "But she never thought Bill took the money."

"We know more than that, Uncle James," said Joe. "We know it has something to do with Bear Trail."

"Do you know what Bear Trail means?" asked Benny.

"Yes, I went over Bear Trail when I was fifteen years old," answered Joe.

"So you did, my boy!" cried Mr. Alden. "On that trail you have to go miles in a canoe, and then carry the canoe. You were very strong when you came back from that first trip."

"I liked it so well that later I was a guide for two years," said Joe. "But I haven't seen Bear Trail for a long time."

"Where is this Bear Trail?" asked Alice.

"Let's go home," said Joe for an answer. "I can show you on the map."

"O.K." said Benny. "I don't think we'll find any more clues in this room."

When they were driving home, Alice said, "I can't think what the little house in Maine means. Bill's yellow house is on Surprise Island."

"We'll have to solve the other mysteries first, I guess," said Henry. "Then maybe we will understand the rest."

"You all sit on the porch while I get the map," said Joe, stopping the station wagon at the front steps.

Soon the map was open on the porch table. The children sat around it. Joe began to point with his pen.

"Bear Trail starts from the highway right here," he said.

"Then you come to a lake. Here it is. There is a camp on this lake. Anyway, there used to be."

"That's where the canoe comes in?" Benny asked.

"Right. It's a beautiful trip. I think I know exactly where to go from here. You paddle the canoe as far as you can. Then you get out and carry the canoe. The woodsmen call that a 'carry.' You can go miles and miles this way. You don't see a house for days."

Henry looked at his grandfather. Jessie did the same. Everyone on the porch was looking at Mr. Alden as he sat in his easy chair.

"Yes, yes! I know what you want!" he said, smiling and nodding his head. "You all want to go up to Maine and hunt for Bill."

"Yes, that's it, Grandfather," said Benny. "But you always let us do things in summer when there isn't any school. Joe and Alice want to go too."

Mr. Alden looked at Joe sharply. "Do you?" he asked.

"Yes, we really do," said Joe, after looking at

Alice. "We both love a mystery. We both love camping and canoeing. Alice is a great paddler in a canoe, and I have two weeks left before I have to go back to work."

"Well, if you want to spend your two weeks that way, it's all right with me," said Mr. Alden at last.

"He means we can all go!" shouted Benny. "Don't you, Grandfather?"

"I suppose so," said Mr. Alden. "You'll have to carry a lot of things with you. Those 'carries' are hard work, my boy."

"Henry's strong," said Benny. "He could carry a lot of things. And so could Alice. She's very strong, too."

"Well, well! Thank you, Benny," said Alice, surprised.

"We'll all be stronger when we get home," said Henry. "I've been wondering what that letter means, Grandfather. Just as Alice said, '*Your* little house in Maine.' His yellow house is on Surprise Island."

"I don't know myself," said Mr. Alden. "But

I know that Bill built the yellow house on Surprise Island. He did all the work himself with the help of his brother."

"Brother? Does this brother have anything to do with this mystery?"

"Yes, I'm afraid so," said Mr. Alden. "I never liked his brother. He was always in trouble."

"You think Bill's brother wrote the letter?" asked Jessie.

"I certainly do," said Mr. Alden. "I think S. M. means Sam McGregor."

"Ho-hum," said Benny.

"Now what does that mean—Ho-hum?" asked Joe, laughing.

"It means we'd better stop talking and get started on this trip," said Benny.

"What a family!" said Joe. "Always doing something exciting."

Mr. Alden said, "You might as well get some of your things ready right away."

"Oh, let's," said Benny, jumping up.

Joe stood up too, and began to think aloud. "We can get two canoes up there," he said slowly. "Do you think you could carry one, Henry, with one of the others to help you?"

"I'm sure I could," said Henry. "We can't take too many things. We'll have to carry food, and packs on our backs, won't we?"

"That's right," said Joe. "We can get tents up there too. There is a store on that first lake where we can buy what food we need for the trip. We don't have to carry the canoes very far."

"We can go to Maine in the station wagon, Joe," said Violet softly.

"Right," said Joe, smiling at his little cousin. "I knew that was a good thing to buy. Now you children get to work and write down the things you want to take. We can get blankets up there, too."

"No, sir! You take blankets from here, Joe," said Mr. Alden suddenly. "Get your clothes and blankets made into packs right here where I can see them. I'm not going to have Violet get cold sleeping in the Maine woods."

Soon there was a great noise around the house. The children ran up and down stairs. Watch went up and down every time. Then Joe showed them how to make sleeping bags. First the blankets were put on the floor and folded once. Then they were sewed on one side to make a bag. Their clothes were put in piles on the blankets.

"Now fold them over and over this way," said Joe, "and put these straps around them. I have a lot more straps in my camping things."

"I see," said Benny. "The strap goes around your back. Mine isn't heavy at all. I could carry some bacon and eggs too."

"Bacon," said Henry, "but no eggs. We can't take eggs, can we, Joe?"

"Not whole eggs," said Joe. "Dried eggs. We can have scrambled eggs. Dried milk and canned milk, both."

"Dried everything," said Benny. "I don't care."

Before night came, the family was ready for the trip.

Then Joe turned to his uncle. "Don't be worried, Uncle James," he said. "I promise you we will stop and eat on the way up. We'll eat well before we go on the canoe trip. Then we will be all right for a few days, if we don't have so much to eat."

"Good," said Mr. Alden. "Everything is ready then."

"No," said Jessie. "Nobody has said anything about Watch."

"Oh, we can't take the dog!" began Joe. "He might tip the canoe over."

Then he looked at the faces of the four children. They were thinking fast. He went on,

"Really, I don't think we had better take Watch."

"You're right, Joe," said Henry at last. "We can't take Watch. But he will have a good time at home."

"Yes," said Mr. Alden. "Watch will keep me from being lonesome, and I will keep him from being lonesome."

Benny made them all feel better by saying, "Let's have him stay home. But don't let's tell him he can't go until tomorrow."

CHAPTER 6

# Starting for Camp

It was a pleasant ride to Maine. They ate lunch on the way. Soon after lunch, Joe turned into a bumpy side road and drove carefully through the woods. Suddenly he pointed ahead to a pretty blue lake on the side of the road. "There is the end of our station wagon ride."

The children looked out as he steered the station wagon up to the door of a little store, and stopped. "All out!" he said.

"Now for the fun!" cried Alice. "What a lot of things we'll buy here!"

The storekeeper came to the door to see who was stopping.

"You don't remember me, Mr. Long," said Joe. "But I was a guide up here once."

"Sure I remember you. You're Joe Alden. Glad to see you. Going on a canoe trip? These all your children?"

"No," laughed Joe. "This is my new wife, and these are my four young cousins."

"How do you do?" said Benny politely. "Oh, Mr. Long, you have canoes over there."

"I have everything for a canoe trip," said Mr. Long with a smile. "Going three in a canoe? I can fix you up all right. You'll need two. You'll need some tents, too."

They all went into the store. "Oh, look!" cried Benny, happily. "All kinds of tin dishes and tin cans. And let's have some pancakes for breakfast!" He took down a box of pancake flour.

"Benny," said Jessie, kindly, "I think you'd

better let Joe tell us what to buy. He knows what we can carry."

"Well, yes, Jessie," said Joe. "But Benny is right about the pancakes. Just wait until you smell them cooking in the early morning."

Mr. Long put the things in a big bag. "Flour, salt, sugar, bacon, dried eggs, canned milk, potatoes, beans, onions, canned fruit," said Alice. "We won't go hungry with that."

"Tin dishes to eat out of and tin dishes to cook in," said Jessie.

They went outdoors to look at canoes.

"I can take care of your station wagon," said

Mr. Long. "Just leave it here." He turned over two canoes and helped Joe push them half into the lake.

Joe thanked him. Then he said, "Just a minute, Mr. Long. We want to ask you something before we go. We are really up here to look for an old man who is lost. He would be about seventy years old now, but he has been lost for almost forty years."

"His name is Bill McGregor," said Benny.

"Never heard of him. I'm sorry," said Mr. Long, shaking his head.

"We're sorry, too," said Violet sadly.

Mr. Long looked at the gentle little girl. "I'll keep my ears open," he said. "I'll let you know if I hear anything about your man."

"Please do," said Joe. "We're about ready."

"I want to go in the canoe with Joe!" cried Benny, jumping up and down.

"Well, you can," said Joe after thinking a minute. "You are light and I am heavy. Henry, I will take Jessie, too. You take Violet and Alice."

"That's nice," said Alice. She smiled at Violet. "I'd like to go with you, and I can help Henry paddle if he needs me."

"I'll put the bag of food, the tent bag, and one blanket roll in the middle of our canoe, Benny," said Joe. "Then you sit down near them and don't move.

"Henry's canoe can carry the other blanket roll and the bag of dishes."

When everything was loaded, Mr. Long gave the canoes a last push into the lake.

"Oh, isn't this lovely!" cried Jessie, as her canoe began to slide through the smooth blue water. "What a beautiful lake this is." She looked back to see Henry taking up his paddle. Then both canoes were on their way.

"Keep near me, Henry," Joe called back. "Then we can shout to each other."

Benny was looking at a spot in the lake. "Is this water very deep, Joe?" he asked.

"Oh, yes, very deep."

"Is it deeper than a tree?" asked Benny, still looking at the spot.

"Oh, yes, much deeper than a tree in the middle," answered Joe laughing. "Why do you ask?"

"Well, there's a tree growing in the lake over there, almost in the middle," cried Benny. "But it's moving!"

"Moving? A tree?" cried Joe. "Why—it's a moose! He's swimming across the lake. Those branches are his antlers, Benny. Hoo-hoo, Henry! Look! A moose!" He pointed at the moose as he shouted to Henry.

But the swimming animal had heard the shouts. He had seen the canoes. He turned around and began to swim as fast as he could toward the shore. When he got near the edge, he splashed through the shallow water and ran out of sight into the bushes.

"Well, well!" said Jessie. "Always something interesting on a canoe trip. Wasn't he a big one, though."

"Keep your eyes open," said Joe. "You may even see a bear."

"Really, Joe?" asked Jessie.

"Well, not right here," answered Joe. "They don't come down here very much. But we may see a bear before we go home."

"And fish!" cried Jessie. "Did you see that fish jump right out of the water?"

"Yes, I did," said Joe. "He was a big fellow."

"Let's go fishing!" cried Benny.

"We can't stop now," said Joe. "We'll have to paddle right along to make camp for the night."

"Are you going to build a fire, Joe?"

Joe smiled. "Yes, indeed," he said. "I can build a fire because I was a guide once. Nobody can build a fire in the Maine woods except a guide."

"I'm glad you're a guide, then," said Benny. "What are you going to cook for supper?"

"A secret," said Joe laughing. "And we may have company. Yes, I think I can promise you company."

"Who in the world could it be?" Jessie asked. "You don't mean Bill, do you?"

"No, not Bill," said Joe quickly.

Then Jessie remembered that Joe had talked quietly with Mr. Long in front of the store. No one else heard a word the two men had said.

"I bet that's a secret, too," said Benny.

"Right," answered Joe.

CHAPTER 7

# Company in the Woods

Henry paddled almost as fast as Joe for about two hours. Then Joe could see that Henry was behind him. "Tired, Henry?" Joe shouted, slowing down and waiting for Henry to catch up.

"A little, Joe," Henry shouted back. "How far is it?"

"Not very far now," said Joe. "Look over there!" He pointed at a spot down the lake. "Three trees! Camp!"

Henry saw the spot at once. "I can paddle that far," he called back.

So they started out once more.

"It will take some time to get the camp ready for the night," Joe told Jessie. "I want to get there long before dark."

"We have to get supper, too," said Benny.

"Don't forget the company," said Joe, winking at Jessie.

Everyone was now looking at the three trees. As they came nearer they could see a beach where canoes could land. Near the beach there was an open place.

Soon, with a strong push of his paddle, Joe sent his canoe up on the beach. Henry's canoe came along beside it, and Joe and Henry jumped out.

They helped everyone out. Then they pulled the two canoes up on the beach almost out of the water, and tied them to a tree.

"So they won't float away," said Benny, watching.

"Take everything out," cried Joe. "Put it in

this open place. Here's one of the best camping places in Maine."

"A long wooden table all made!" cried Henry. "And places to sit. That's good."

"What a nice smell here," said Violet to Alice. "I just love the smell of evergreen trees. It makes me think of the dear old boxcar days."

"I don't see any company, though," said Benny, looking around.

"Well, you will," said Joe. He seemed to be very sure. "The first thing will be a campfire because we are so hungry. The next thing will be the tents, because we will soon be sleepy."

He took out an axe. "Here is a path. We'll follow it and cut down two small trees, *not* evergreens though. These trees must be just right. Look at this picture. See, the top must have a fork. But the fork must be one-sided, so we can drive the tree into the ground."

All four children looked at the picture, and started to walk down the path.

"Wait a minute," said Joe. "There is something else we must find. Do you see the pail hanging over the fire on a long branch? We must have a long branch like that, with a fork at the top, and another to hang our water pail on."

"But trees don't grow like that," said Jessie. "All branches grow one way, don't they, Joe?"

"You just look around," said Joe, smiling. "You might find one."

First the children began to look for a tree that was not an evergreen. It was Violet who saw the first one. Joe said the fork was just right. Henry began to cut it down. Jessie and Benny soon found another just like it.

"Joe! Wait! I hear something," called Jessie suddenly.

They all stood still and listened. Far in the woods they heard someone whistling. Joe laughed. "Company!" he said.

The whistling came nearer. "Hi!" shouted Joe.

"Hi!" answered a deep voice. Just then, the children saw a white-haired man in a brown coat, carrying a very large pack. His face was brown from the sun, his blue eyes were kind.

"This is Mr. Hill, children," said Joe, smiling at the stranger. "Mr. Long tells me he is one of the best guides in Maine."

"Well, I wouldn't say that," laughed the man. "I suppose you are Joe Alden. Want me to build your shelter-half and cook you some cornbread?"

"Cornbread!" cried Alice. "I just love cornbread."

"Me too!" shouted Benny. "But what's a shelter-half?"

"You *would* ask that, Benny," said Henry laughing. "But we don't know, either."

"No," cried Benny, "don't tell us after all, Mr. Hill. We'll watch you build it, and then we'll know what it is."

"Not a bad idea," said Henry. "Don't forget we still have to find that branch with two forks in it."

Mr. Hill could see two or three branches like that, but he said nothing. He just smiled and let the children find a tree for themselves.

"Well, well!" said Henry at last, looking up at

a tree. "There *is* a branch growing both ways. I never knew they grew like that."

"Cut it just below that fork, Henry," said Joe.

Soon the branch was cut. Joe and Henry cut branches of evergreens and carried them back to camp for beds.

Then Mr. Hill and Joe put everyone to work. "We must get everything done before the sun sets," said Mr. Hill. "It gets very cold up here at night. You'll be glad of your warm blanket rolls. Benny–is that your name? You come and hold these two trees for me."

In no time the two little forked trees were standing in the ground with a long pole between them. The branch was soon hooked over the pole. Mr. Hill put the water pail on the hook. "You can push this branch to one side, you see," he said. "Sometimes I get two or three to cook with."

"I can see how that works," said Benny. "The water gets hot while you cook supper."

"Is the hot water to wash dishes in?" asked Violet.

"That's right, and for anything else you want to wash."

"Maybe hands," said Henry, laughing and looking at his hands.

"It's good clean dirt, though," said Benny, looking at his own hands. "Smells good. Just like evergreens." Then he forgot all about his hands, for Mr. Hill began to make the shelter-half to keep the wind from the fire.

"This would keep rain out, too, if we had any rain," he said to Benny. "And this is the baker where we cook the cornbread."

"Oh, that's a funny dish," said Benny. "How does it work?"

Mr. Hill laughed. "You set it up with this open side toward the fire, see? The inside gets very hot, and cooks the cornbread a fine even brown on top. Then after supper, we can set it up on this other end, and wash dishes in it."

"Well, isn't that clever?" cried Henry. "Benny won't mind washing dishes in that."

"Now somebody had better go and find some wood," said Mr. Hill. "We must get a fire going right away."

Benny jumped up and worked hard getting wood for the fire. He was getting hungry.

Meanwhile Joe and Henry put up the two small tents. Alice and Jessie laid the evergreen branches in the tents for beds.

"Where will Mr. Hill sleep?" asked Jessie.

"Oh, he has his own tent," Joe answered. "It will take him about one minute to put his tent up and make his bed and go sound asleep."

"I hope he won't go to sleep before he makes that cornbread," said Alice.

"We're going to have ham and eggs, too," said Mr. Hill.

"But we haven't any eggs," said Benny.

"No, but I have," said Mr. Hill with a laugh. "I brought along a few things. Just for your first day. Then tomorrow morning I have to leave you."

How delicious the ham did smell when Mr. Hill put it in the big pan and it began to get brown. Then he dropped in twelve eggs. Joe said he could eat at least two, while Henry said he could eat three.

"Real butter!" cried Jessie, as Mr. Hill took it out. "Do you remember the first time we had real butter in the boxcar?"

"Cornbread isn't much good without butter," said Mr. Hill.

Violet began to set the table with tin plates. Soon they were all eating their first meal in camp.

At last Joe said, "The cornbread is gone and the ham is gone. Can anyone stay awake long enough to wash the dishes?"

"I can, if we can use that funny dish," said Benny. He watched Mr. Hill put the hot water from the pail into the baker. "But I'm so sleepy I could go to sleep standing up."

Soon the dishes were washed and put away.

Alice, Violet and Jessie had one tent, and Henry, Joe, and Benny had the other. They spread their blanket rolls on the beds of evergreen boughs. Before long the moon looked down on a sleeping camp.

But softly through the woods walked a large black animal. He smelled people. He smelled food, too. So he walked very quietly.

There was the side of bacon hanging in a tree, up high. That was easy. He could stand up. Maybe he could pull it down. He loved bacon. Up went one front paw and the bacon began to swing back and forth.

The animal was not the only one awake. Mr. Hill had heard the visitor. This was the very minute he had been waiting for. "Joe!" he called from his own tent. "We have a visitor."

Joe woke up suddenly. "I'll tell the children,"

he answered. "Henry, wake up!" Then Henry was awake. "Jessie!" he whispered. Then everyone was awake.

"Oh, dear!" said Violet sitting up. "What is it?"

CHAPTER 8

# The Lumber Camp

The moon was almost as bright as day.

Mr. Hill whispered, "Look out very quietly." Very slowly the other tent flaps opened.

The children saw the large black bear but he did not hear them or smell them. He did not smell anything but the bacon. Back and forth it swung as he hit it with his big paw.

"Don't be afraid, Violet," whispered Alice. "The bear won't hurt us. He is afraid of us."

Just then the bacon fell at the bear's feet. Down he went on all fours again. He lay down and began to chew the bacon.

"Ho-hum!" thought Benny. "There goes our bacon."

Just then Mr. Hill flashed a light in the bear's face. The bear jumped up and ran off into the woods as fast as he could run.

"Didn't he look funny!" laughed Benny. "But he left our bacon."

"That was a wonderful sight," said Henry. "I am certainly glad that Mr. Hill happened to wake up."

They were soon asleep again. They did not know that Joe had asked Mr. Hill to come because he could show them a big black bear. They did not know that Mr. Hill and the bear were good friends. The bear knew that he would find food wherever Mr. Hill was.

The next morning Mr. Hill said as he and Joe made a fire, "I must leave you after breakfast. When you start off, you'll soon come to a lumber camp."

"I wish you would leave that baker to wash dishes in," said Benny.

"Yes, I brought it for you," said Mr. Hill with

a smile. He washed the bacon well, and cut it in thin pieces. Soon it was cooking in the pan over the fire. Hot cereal and canned milk seemed delicious in the cold morning air. Mr. Hill made "quick bread" in the little baker. As soon as the bread was done, the children began to hear many bluejays in the trees.

"They want our breakfast," said Mr. Hill, looking up. "Wait until we sit down and then see how near they will come. Throw some pieces on the ground."

The air was full of bluejays. Six or seven beautiful birds flew to the ground. The children could almost touch them.

"Come on, everybody," said Benny at last. "I want to see that lumber camp." He began to pick up the dishes, making the birds fly back into the trees.

Jessie laughed. "What a housekeeper you are all of a sudden," she said. "Let's all help."

Soon the camp was all clean again. Everything was packed in the canoes, and Mr. Hill gave them each a push.

"Thanks, Mr. Hill," said Joe to his old friend.

"Thanks for everything," Jessie called back as the two canoes went smoothly down the lake.

The children waved until Mr. Hill turned and went into the woods.

"He was nice, wasn't he?" said Violet.

"All Maine guides are nice, Violet," laughed Joe.

Fish were jumping here and there in the water beside the canoes.

"Oh, can't we go fishing today, Joe?" asked Benny.

"We'll have to go fishing," said Joe, "unless we want to eat beans for three days. When we get around two or three 'looks' we'll stop and fish."

"Two or three what?" asked Benny.

"Looks," replied Joe. "See that turn in the lake? You can't see around it yet. They call that a look."

"That's a good name for it," said Jessie. "What do we fish with?"

"Didn't you see the fishing rods Mr. Hill brought us?" asked Benny. "He brought two, one for each canoe. We can take turns fishing."

"We fish with flies," Joe told them. "Not real flies. I have a box of Grey Ghosts in my pack. They look like real flies to the fish. So they go after them and get caught."

The canoes passed the next look and the next. Then Joe called back to Henry, "Want to stop and fish?"

"You bet!" called Henry. "You'll have to show us how."

"Alice knows how," called Joe. He stopped paddling. "She'll show you and Violet."

The two canoes floated together as Joe and Alice each put a pretty Grey Ghost fly on their lines. Then Joe whipped his line out over the water.

"That's nice, Joe," cried Benny. "Isn't it easy? When you get a fish, let me try, will you?"

"Sure," said Joe, smiling. "Sit very still now."

"Oh, look," cried Jessie. "You've got a fish, Alice! Pull it in!"

"Not so fast," answered Alice. "You have to play these fellows." She pulled her line in very slowly and carefully. Everyone watched her land the large fish and take it off the hook.

Then Joe caught one. Benny could hardly wait.

"Now it's my turn," he cried.

"Right," said Joe. "You saw me whip the line over the water. Now you do it."

Benny took the rod. He lifted it just as Joe had done. "Whip!" went the line. But it did not go out over the water. It went backwards over his head.

"Look *out!*" cried Joe to Alice. But he was too late. The hook caught fast in her hair and pulled it down over her face.

"Oh, Alice, your pretty smooth hair!" said Violet.

"I'm sorry, Alice!" called Benny. "I don't see how I did that."

"Never mind," said Alice. "I ought to have been watching. Everyone misses the first time. Violet will soon get the hook out."

Violet leaned over at once and worked the hook out. "Don't do that again, Benny," she said.

"It's not as easy as it looks, Benny, to whip that line out," said Jessie. "You'd better let Joe do the fishing."

"No, not at all," Joe answered. "Let him try again. He ought to learn."

Benny fished and fished. But he found it worth while when he caught three trout. He looked at every spot on the fish as if he had made it himself.

At last Joe said, "We have enough fish now. The men at the lumber camp will want to feed us. But it's nice to have our own food, too."

"See the logs in the water over there," said Alice. "The men at the camp roll the logs into the water and they float down by themselves."

When the children started off again, they began to hear the sound of axes. Soon they could hear a great crash when a tree fell. At last they heard a lumber man calling to them, "Hi! Hi!"

They all waved to him. "Paddle in, Henry," said Joe. "We'll stay here tonight."

The man seemed very glad to see them. Right away he asked them to stay to dinner.

"Yes, we'll be glad to," said Joe. "We have a lot of fish here, but we'd like to put up our tents in your camp for the night."

"Fine!" said the man, who was the boss. "Hi, Cookie! We have company."

The cook looked up with a laugh. "Come in! Stay as long as you want. You like beans?"

Benny went up to the cook. "We just love beans," he said. "But we got a lot of fish. I'll show you the ones I caught."

"You can't tell them apart," said Henry.

"Oh, yes, I can," said Benny. "I caught three, and I know every one. I caught this one, and this one, and this one!"

"They look just alike to me," said Cookie, with a smile.

"Cook them for the little boy, Cookie," said the boss. "Fix them all up."

When dinner was ready, Cookie let Benny ring the bell. The lumber men came crashing through the bushes.

"They always hurry that way to their dinner," said Cookie.

The men made room for the visitors. There were three tables full of people. Baked beans and quick bread made a fine dinner.

After dinner the boss said, "You show the visitors how we cut the trees, Bill."

"Bill!" whispered Violet to Joe. They all looked to see which man was Bill. But they knew right off it was not the Bill they were hunting for. He was too young.

The afternoon went by too quickly. After a supper of their cooked fish, they went to bed in their own tents. The lumber men had little log houses.

"Don't be surprised if you hear porcupines,"

said the boss. "They like the grease around here, and they come most every night."

"What do they sound like?" asked Henry.

"Like pigs," said the boss. "They squeal and they chew. When they chew it sounds like someone sawing wood."

When the camp was quiet Henry woke up suddenly. He thought it was morning and the men were sawing. Then he heard many loud squeals, and said to himself, "It's porcupines!"

But the squeals had wakened all the rest, and both tent doors opened.

"What a noise," whispered Jessie. "Where are they?"

"See that ball?" asked Alice. "Right by the table? That is a porcupine. He is chewing the table to get the grease."

There were five porcupines in all, eating and squealing. When the children had watched them for a long time, Joe said, "We must get our sleep. They'd better go." Then he flashed a light at them. They rolled into balls and kept very still.

But when Joe flashed the light again, they went hurrying away into the woods.

"Well," said Jessie, lying down again, "we see our most interesting sights in the middle of the night."

"I hope they won't come back," said Alice. "Because Joe says tomorrow will be a hard day."

But even Joe had no idea how hard the next day was going to be.

CHAPTER 9

# Almost Starving

After the day in the lumber camp, the morning seemed to come in no time. Then men were awake and working before the sun. When everyone was dressed, Joe took the children to find the boss.

"I wonder if you ever heard of a man named Bill McGregor," he said to the boss.

"He's lost," said Benny.

"Lost? How old a man?"

"About seventy, now," answered Joe. "He

has been gone for many years. But we just found a letter saying he might have gone on Bear Trail."

"This is part of Bear Trail," said the boss.

"Yes, I know," said Joe. "That's why we came. This Bill was a very strong man, so I thought maybe he had worked years ago in lumber camps."

"Well, I'll ask my men," said the boss. "I'll find a way to let you know if I hear anything."

"We are going to stop at Old Village," said Joe. "If you do hear anything about this man, send someone down by canoe. I'll pay for it."

"I guess not!" laughed the boss. "Too bad if I couldn't help you out. I'll be glad to let you know anything I hear. You have two looks and a carry before you get to Old Village Lake."

"Breakfast!" called Cookie, ringing the bell. Soon the men were eating great plates of quick bread. But Cookie had made beautiful brown pancakes for the visitors. They ate them with butter and brown sugar.

"I'll help paddle today, Henry," said Alice.

"Thanks," said Henry. "We'll get along faster that way."

After breakfast everything was packed up again and put in the canoes. The children did not forget to thank Cookie and the kind lumber boss. Very soon they were on their way down the lake. The day was beautiful. They saw two interesting things. They paddled around the first look and saw a moose swimming to shore as fast as he could. Around the next look they saw a beautiful deer standing in the bushes.

"I like to go around these looks," cried Benny. "I'm glad we came. Now what's next, Joe?"

"Well," answered Joe with a funny smile, "soon we'll get out and carry the canoes." He winked at Jessie.

"Can I carry one?" asked Benny.

"No, certainly not," said Joe. "Henry and Alice will carry one with the things still in it. That will be right side up. Then I will carry the other upside down on my head. You and Violet will have to carry some bags. Not as much fun as you think.

"You see this lake stops just ahead. But there is a very big lake not far from here. That's the last lake for us."

Henry and Joe soon pulled both canoes up on the shore. Alice took one end of a canoe under her arm, and Henry took the other. Benny laughed and laughed as Joe put the other canoe upside down on his head and walked off down the path. Benny and Violet came after with the bags.

It was not very far, and Alice was glad, because the canoe was heavy. Everyone sat down by the next lake to rest.

"What a beautiful day this is!" cried Jessie. She could not help it. The lake was the biggest one they had seen. The water was very blue and the trees were very dark green.

"Let's rest a long time," said Joe. "We have a long canoe trip ahead of us. There are not many good places to land for dinner."

But at last he got up and they were on their way again. This time they did not paddle out to the middle of the lake. It was too far.

"Stay near land, Henry," said Joe. "Then we won't have so far to paddle." But when he said this, he did not know how lucky they were going to be.

The two canoes were going along smoothly. Nobody thought of rain. Suddenly Joe looked up at the sky.

"Look up, Henry!" he called.

Just at that minute the wind began to blow. All of a sudden the smooth lake was very black. Soon it was all covered with small waves, then big ones.

For one long minute Joe stopped paddling and looked sharply along the shore. "Get to shore, Henry!" he shouted. "Just as fast as you can! Land between those two large trees." He had to shout, for the wind was making a terrible noise.

They turned both canoes. By now they could hardly sit up. Alice paddled without a word. Henry's canoe went first. Then it began to rain. The rain fell so fast that in one minute they were all wet through. But they thought of nothing but getting to shore.

"You can make it, Henry!" yelled Joe. "There is room for us both to land. Get over to one side!"

Henry and Alice paddled under the branches of the two trees and drove their canoe up into a very small opening.

"Get out quickly!" cried Alice. "Pull our canoe out of Joe's way, so he can land, too." They did so. Even Violet helped. Then they waved to Joe.

"O.K!" he shouted as he began to paddle straight in. Just then a big wave hit his canoe sideways and washed the bags of food and dishes into the lake.

"Never *mind!*" he yelled. "Let them go, Benny, and sit still!"

Then with one strong push he drove his canoe up beside Henry's. He looked at his young wife, who was very white.

"Thank goodness!" said Alice. "We are all safe!" She put her arm around Violet who was shaking with fright.

"We'll have to do something right away,"

said Henry, taking one look at his gentle little sister. "We're really in a fix. All our food is gone."

"Are we going to starve, Joe?" asked Benny.

"Starve? No. But I guess we are going to be very hungry."

"Just *almost* starve," said Benny.

"Let's not stand here in the rain talking," said Jessie. "We still have our tents and our blankets. And we still have our shelter-half. We must think of some way to get Violet dry and warm."

"I'm all right," said Violet. But she did not look all right. She was still shaking.

Henry and Joe looked around. They could see nothing but trees and bushes. There was no path. There was no other open place.

"Not a very good place to land, or make a camp," said Henry, much worried.

"All woods and bushes," said Benny. "But we could cut down some trees and bushes. We still have our axe."

"Thank goodness for that," said Henry. "Let's have it."

"Don't cut here," said Joe. "The ground is too wet for a camp. Let's try to find a better place. You go that way, Henry, and I'll go this. Hunt around, and don't get lost."

Before long they both came crashing back. But now Joe was smiling.

"Water!" he shouted. "There's a spring up there, and quite a good place. We can make it do. We'll have to. We won't need to cut down many bushes and there is room for the tents and a fire."

"How can you build a fire in the rain?" asked Benny.

"Don't forget we have the shelter-half," said Joe. "You bring in some big stones and some dry wood, and you'll see."

"All the wood is wet," said Benny.

"Not on the under side it isn't," Henry told him. "Look at Jessie, with that axe!"

As fast as Jessie cut down bushes, Alice pulled them away. Joe and Henry put up Mr. Hill's shelter-half as fast as they could. Soon Joe had a fire going. He made Violet sit down before it, putting a blanket over her knees.

"Thank you, Joe," said the little girl. "The fire feels so nice and warm." She did not shake any more.

"Good!" cried Henry. "That shelter-half is wonderful. It keeps the wind off the fire, too."

"Can I go back to the canoes and see if I can find any food?" asked Benny.

"Good boy!" said Joe. "A fine idea. You may be a Maine guide yet."

"I'll go with you, Benny," said Alice suddenly, after a look at Joe. "We might even get hold of one bag."

Off they went, while Joe and Henry put up the tents. The big trees kept off a lot of the rain, and the inside of the tents was quite dry.

Jessie took the blanket rolls inside before she took off the straps. "Anyway," she said, "we have a warm, dry place to sleep, even if we don't have anything to eat."

Joe was thinking. He was worried. He knew it would be hard for the children to go a whole day and night without eating.

Meanwhile two people were really having fun —Alice and Benny. They could see the one bag of food as it lay under the water not far from shore. The wind was blowing so hard that every wave brought the bag nearer to them.

"If I could only get hold of it!" said Benny. "It has potatoes and tin cans in it. Let's have the fishing rod."

"You'd break it," said Alice. "Here's a long stick."

"Please let me walk into the lake, Alice," begged Benny. "I'm as wet as I can be already. I don't have to go in very far."

"Well, all right," said Alice slowly. "It isn't very deep here. Go easy, now."

What a funny feeling that was. Benny stepped into the lake very slowly. He went in up to his knees. He had the big stick in one hand and he held the branches of the trees with the other. He tried and tried to get hold of the bag. He did not give up until he had hooked the stick into the handle of the bag. Then he pulled carefully. The bag almost floated. Then he caught it with his hand and pulled it to shore.

"Oh, *Benny*, dear!" cried Alice. She was so

glad she almost cried. "How glad Joe will be!"

They both took hold of the bag and pulled it to camp.

"Look here!" shouted Benny. "Potatoes!"

"Wonderful! Potatoes!" they all said. They opened the bag and took out what was left. Their flour was gone, the salt was gone, the sugar was gone. But there were the potatoes and all the cans of milk.

"No dishes," said Benny. "They were all in the other bag."

"Never mind dishes!" cried Violet. "Just think of having potatoes, Benny. We can cook potatoes without any dishes."

It was long past noon, and everyone began to work.

"Roll the potatoes into the fire, right here," said Joe. "They will burn, but never mind. We have to eat something. We can put spring water in the milk and drink that, too."

"How can we put spring water into a can of milk?" Benny asked. "It's full of milk already."

Henry had an idea. He rushed off to his own

canoe. Soon he was back with the water pail and his big knife. "Now we've got a dish," he said. "We can put the milk and water in this pail, and we'll open the milk cans with this knife."

"Then the cans will be empty," broke in Benny.

"And we can use them for cups," finished Jessie.

"Well," said Benny, "anyway, we're not starving. Just almost starving."

CHAPTER 10

# Potato Camp

"It's better to lose the food than the tents, isn't it, Joe?" asked Jessie.

"It certainly is," answered Joe, feeding the fire. "We will get along all right for one night. This rain will stop as suddenly as it began. I think by tomorrow morning we can get back on the lake."

Jessie thought that out. "Does that mean we must have dinner, and supper and breakfast here, Joe?"

Joe winked at her. "Right," he said. "But I guess we won't have much breakfast."

"Let's eat half the potatoes for dinner and the rest for supper," said Jessie, thinking. "But we have no butter, and no salt. Just potatoes."

"Better than nothing, Jess," said Henry, looking at his sister. "You always make the best of things. Now, let's get lots of wood. We can't get much wetter. Then when we do get dry, we won't have to go out in the rain again."

By the time the potatoes were done, there was a big pile of wood in Joe's tent and there were six hungry people sitting by the fire.

With a long stick, Joe and Henry pulled the potatoes out of the fire.

"Two each," said Jessie. She gave them out. That is, she rolled two potatoes to each one. "Now let's put the canned milk in the water pail with some spring water."

"What a dinner!" cried Benny. "I don't like canned milk when I'm home. But it tastes all right here."

It was certainly queer not to have any dishes

except a water pail and milk cans. But even as the wind kept on blowing and the rain kept on falling, everyone was very happy to have tin cups and a water pail.

"We are pretty lucky to have anything to eat," said Violet. "If you hadn't found the bag, Benny, we wouldn't be eating now."

The children opened the hot potatoes with sticks. They ate them with small sticks.

"Awfully hot, aren't they?" said Henry, burning his fingers. "But aren't they delicious!"

"We have to eat slowly this time," said Joe. "Make them last as long as you can."

"No dishes to wash," said Benny. "Too bad we lost that funny little baker."

Then Joe said, "Let me tell you just what we have to do, children."

Everyone looked up and listened.

"This is a very long lake as you see," began Joe. "But if we start very early tomorrow morning, we ought to get to the end of our trip before noon."

"Where do we come out, Joe?" asked Jessie.

"We come out in a very small village," answered Joe. "When I was here, there were only a few houses and a store."

"What is the name of this place?" asked Henry.

"I don't think it has any real name," said Joe, thinking. "They just call it Old Village. Most of it is very old. Only one or two houses were built when the Indians lived there."

"After we get to Old Village, you don't know where to go next?" asked Benny.

"No, I don't," said Joe. "That is the end of Bear Trail."

"Well, never mind," said Henry. "Something is sure to happen. We may find the tin box, or even Bill. I can hardly wait to find clues."

Joe did not answer. He was thinking.

"I do wish we had saved some of our fish from yesterday," said Jessie. "We had enough left to go with our potatoes for supper."

"That's all right, Jessie," said Benny, taking his last drink of milk. "I'm not hungry at all."

They all laughed. "That's because you have just eaten your dinner," said Violet. "You'll be hungry again at supper time, and then again at breakfast."

"O.K." said Benny. "Then I suppose we'll really starve without any breakfast at all."

"Not quite," said Alice, smiling at the boy.

The wind was still blowing and the rain still came down. The children put sticks on the fire, and drank the spring water in the pail. Jessie had washed out the tin cans and they drank water because the milk was all gone.

After a supper of potatoes, they were all glad to go to bed. They were still hungry, but they were warm and dry.

From his tent Joe called goodnight to the girls. Then he said, "Notice the wind."

"What's the matter with the wind, Joe?" asked Benny sitting up. "Oh, I see what you mean. There isn't any."

"That's right," said Joe, laughing. "It has just stopped blowing. Tomorrow will be a fine day, I think. Just you wait and see."

But Benny sat up again. He called out, "Hi, Jessie!"

"What do you want, Benny?" Jessie called back.

"Let's call this Potato Camp, because we didn't eat anything here but potatoes." After that, the children always called it Potato Camp.

CHAPTER 11

# Old Village

The next day was fine, just as Joe had said. It was so fine that the children could hardly believe there had been such a storm. But how hungry they were!

"No breakfast today," Joe called in a loud voice. "Think you can take it?"

"Oh, sure," said Benny. "But I hope we can have some dinner."

"Well, I think we can," said Joe. "We can surely find something to eat when we get to Old Village."

"That's where we'll find Bill," said Benny happily.

Henry and Alice started with a will to take down the tents. Violet and Benny began to roll up their blankets. But Joe did nothing. He sat down on a log and seemed to be thinking. This was not like Joe at all.

"Let him alone," said Alice quietly to the children. "Just go on packing. He'll soon help, too."

But Joe didn't begin to pack. Instead he called them all to stop packing and come to him for a minute.

"I want you all to understand why I took you way up here," he said. "Maybe for nothing. Benny just said, 'That's where we'll find Bill.' Now I don't really think we will find Bill. I never thought so. I think Bill must have died long ago. The boss at the lumber camp had never heard of him. Mr. Long and Mr. Hill hadn't either and they both have been around here many years."

Joe stopped and smiled at Benny. Then he

went on. "I don't *really* think we'll find the tin box either."

"Why are you telling us all this, Joe?" asked Violet in her gentle voice. "Are you afraid we'll be disappointed?"

"You're exactly right!" said Joe quickly. He looked at his little cousin. "I don't want you to be disappointed because you can't solve the mystery. When we get to Old Village, I don't know what to do next. I thought maybe we might get a clue to the tin box, but we may not."

"I don't care, Joe," shouted Benny. "I've had enough fun just camping, even if we don't find Bill."

"Oh, yes, we've all had fun, Joe," Jessie broke in.

Joe's face brightened. "Did you really?" he asked. "Even if we don't find a thing? I hope so. That's why I brought you so far. I thought we'd have fun anyway."

"Don't you worry any more, Joe," said Henry. "Camping is the thing we like to do best in the world. It makes us think of Boxcar days and last summer on Surprise Island. But you don't mind if we still look for clues, do you?"

"Mind—no!" said Joe. "I expect to look for clues myself. Just don't be disappointed, that's all."

Then Joe hurried around and began to pack with a will. This time the children were glad to see a smile on his face.

"We'll paddle faster today," he told them, "because we are so hungry. We can't see Old Village from here, because the lake turns. But we ought to get there by noon."

Into the canoes went the things again, and into the canoes went the six people. Off they went on the last part of their long journey. They paddled for a long time.

All at once Benny asked, "Joe, what would happen if I put a Grey Ghost fly on a line and threw it in the water behind the canoe?"

"Well," answered Joe smiling, "you might lose your rod, and then again you might catch a fish." He was delighted to give Benny something to do. Then the boy would not feel so hungry.

"I'm going to try it," said Benny. This time he put on the fly right. Then he threw the line out behind the canoe.

"What are you trying to do? Break your rod?" shouted Henry from the other canoe.

"No," called Benny. "I'm fishing."

On they went. Benny watched his line for a while.

Suddenly Henry shouted, "There goes your rod!"

Benny jumped and caught it just as it was about to slide out of the canoe.

"Boy! You've got a big one," cried Joe, stopping to look back. "Pull him in slowly, Ben! Don't you lose him! Don't get excited, whatever you do!"

Violet smiled. Joe was as excited as Benny.

How the big fish did fight to get away! But Benny played him carefully, and slowly brought him to the side of the canoe.

"Want me to help, young fellow?" asked Joe.

"Please," said Benny. He was afraid he would lose the big fish.

Joe leaned out and pulled it quickly into the canoe.

"A big lake trout! And a beauty," he cried. "He will feed us all. Too bad you didn't catch him yesterday."

"Isn't that always the way!" cried Benny. "We starved yesterday, and now just as we get near a store, we catch a fish."

"Never mind," said Joe. "We'll eat him yet."

He took up his paddle again. It was almost noon when they went around the last look. Then they could see a road that came right down to the beach from Old Village.

"Here we are at the end of Bear Trail," Alice said, laughing; "and we have found neither a clue nor Bill. Joe, aren't you excited now?"

"Excited? Yes, I am," said Joe. "I'm hungry, too. Look ahead at the beach. See that man waiting to meet us? Someone always meets canoes."

Joe and Henry paddled faster without knowing it. Soon the canoes slid up on the beach. The man helped pull up the canoes.

"Hello, strangers," he said. "Taking the Bear Trail trip?"

"Yes," said Joe. "Right now we are looking for some place to eat. These children are almost starved. Is there any place to eat in Old Village?"

"Yes, sir!" said the man. "I run it myself. I call it Jim's Place. I'm Jim Carr. I'll cook you anything you want. Bacon, ham, deer, hamburger—"

"Oh, *hamburger!*" yelled Benny. "I want hamburger!"

"So do I," laughed Jessie.

Jim laughed too. "Leave your things," he said. "Nobody will take them. My place is right up on the road."

The children saw it at once. There was a board over the door, saying in black letters, JIM'S PLACE. They all walked down the road toward it.

"I suppose most of the campers eat with you?" asked Joe.

"Right," said Jim. "They stay overnight sometimes. Then they go back to Mr. Long's store by road."

"We may do that," said Joe.

Jim's Place was the biggest house in Old Village. As they went in, they looked around. Everything was very clean. There were three tables, and a delicious smell of onions in the air.

"I won't be long," said Jim. "Sit down and make yourselves at home. Hamburger and onions and potatoes for everybody."

They sat down and looked at each other. They could hardly wait. Soon Jim came in with big white plates filled with hot food. "Eat all you want," he said. "More in the kitchen. I just made two big apple pies. Maybe I can find some cheese to go with it."

Everyone began to eat. Never did food seem so good to the hungry children. "You see, we didn't have any breakfast," Benny said to Jim.

Jim laughed.

"That's really true," said Joe. "We got caught in the rain, and lost most of our food."

"Too bad," said Jim. He went into the kitchen to get a pie. Soon a whole pie had disappeared, and also some fine yellow cheese he had found.

"Oh, I do feel better," cried Violet. "I'm ready for anything."

"Glad to hear that," said Henry, looking at her. "You do look a little better."

Then Alice said to Joe, "We ought to stay in Old Village for one night, anyway. I think Violet ought to sleep in a bed in a house."

"You can do that all right," answered Jim Carr with a laugh. "You see that little old house across the street? I don't really own it, but I take care of it. It has been empty for many years. When campers want to stay overnight, I let them use it. I bought a lot of folding cots. The campers don't seem to mind sleeping three in a room."

Jessie stopped to count. "We wouldn't either," she said.

"Right!" said Alice with a smile at Jessie. "You and Violet and I in one room, and Joe and Henry and Benny in another."

"There are two rooms," said Jim. "Three with the kitchen."

Henry said, "My! Everything is working out

well, isn't it, Joe? Is there anything interesting to see in Old Village, Jim?"

"Oh, yes," said Jim smiling. "Some people go hunting for deer and moose. Then there's an old hermit over in the woods. Lives all alone. People like to catch sight of him, he looks so queer with his long white beard. Then there are Indians up the road. They make baskets to sell. People always go and watch them make baskets when they stop over."

"Oh, let's go up and see the Indians," said Jessie. "Do they mind? Are they old?"

"No, they don't mind. They like it. Yes, one of them is very old. He has lived there all his life. Loves to talk."

"Ho-hum," said Benny looking at Henry.

"That's what I say too," said Henry softly to Benny. "You mean the old Indian might give us a clue?"

"Maybe," said Benny, smiling to himself.

Henry paid for their dinner, and they all went off up the road.

"Joe," began Jessie, excitedly, "maybe this

old Indian has heard of Bill, long ago. We can ask him."

Soon they could see an Indian girl sitting on the steps of an old house making a basket.

"My, doesn't she work fast!" said Alice. "See her fingers fly."

"I wish I could learn to do that," said Violet.

"You can. I will teach you," said the Indian girl who had heard every word. "It is not hard at all. See, I have just started this basket. See—I go in and out, over and under, with this sweet grass."

The girl worked slowly so that Violet could

see what she did. Soon she held out the basket. "You try it now," she said.

Violet took the basket, and soon her clever fingers were going in and out, over and under, just as the Indian girl had done.

"Wonderful, Violet!" said Alice. "You can do anything with your fingers."

"Yes, she can," said Henry smiling. Then he thought surely Benny would say something about his sister Violet as he always did.

He looked around. But Benny was nowhere to be seen.

"Oh, *where* is Benny?" he called.

"Benny! Ben-*ny!*" shouted Joe as loud as he could.

But there was no answer. Benny had disappeared.

CHAPTER 12

# A Hunt for Benny

It was true. Benny was not there.

"Oh, what has happened to Benny?" said Jessie, beginning to cry.

"Now, don't let's get upset," said Joe's strong voice. "I think I know what has happened. Benny has gone off by himself to find the hermit. He hasn't been gone long, and we can surely find him. Don't you cry, Jessie. We'll go and hunt for him."

"Wouldn't we save time by asking Jim?" asked Henry.

"Right," said Joe. With that, they all ran back to Jim's Place.

Jim came to the door when he saw them running toward him.

"We've lost Benny!" cried Jessie. "You know which way to hunt, don't you? We think he went to find the hermit and surprise us."

"Well, now," said Jim, "the first thing, don't you get scared. We've got Indians here in Old Village that can find anything in these woods. The little boy hasn't been gone long. Did you ask the little Indian girl to help you?"

"Oh, dear," said Violet. "I forgot all about the Indian girl. I just dropped the basket and ran. We all did."

"Better go back, then," said Jim. "I'll go with you. Rita is a better guide than I am. She can walk in the woods and never make a sound."

When Jim told Rita, she stood up at once and looked sharply into the woods. "I saw the little boy at first," she said. "But I did not notice when he went. I'm very sorry. We'll start this way."

Rita leaned over and looked at a bush. "Yes, I think he went down this path. Keep right behind me. It is easy to get lost in these woods if you get off the path."

It was a strange sight—six people walking behind the Indian girl in a straight line down the path. Sometimes it seemed as if there were no path at all.

Jessie walked just behind Rita. Soon she said, "Rita, Benny would never know this was a path. He may have gone off it long ago."

"No, he couldn't, a little boy like that," said Rita. "He couldn't get through. This is the only way he could go. He went this way all right. I can see where he stepped, and this is the way to the old hermit's cabin."

On they went, over rocks and stones and branches.

"Now, call him," said Rita, turning around.

Henry put his hands up like a cup and called "Ben-*ny!*"

Then Joe did the same.

They all listened. There was no answer.

"We'll find him just the same," said Rita shaking her head. "If I can't, my father can."

They all hurried on. For a long time they walked without talking.

Suddenly the Indian girl stopped. "Be careful now," she said. "We are near the hermit's cabin. If we scare him, the hermit will run away, and then he won't help us."

Slowly and quietly they all walked along the path. Then all at once they saw the cabin. They stopped. For on the steps sat an old man with a long white beard. Beside him, smiling and talking away happily, sat Benny.

"Oh, *Benny!*" whispered Jessie.

"Sh!" said Rita.

But the hermit had seen them. "Come," he said to Benny, taking his hand. "You are lost."

Jessie could not wait. She cried out, "Oh, Benny, you scared us so!" With that, everyone began to talk to Benny, so nobody could understand a word.

"The hermit is nice," said Benny when he

could make them hear. "He was going to take me back when I got ready to go. His name is Dave Hunter."

"That's right," said Jim. "His name is Dave Hunter."

But the hermit surprised them all by turning his back. He went straight back to his cabin, went in, and shut the door.

"That's the way he is," said Jim. "He won't talk."

"He talked to me," said Benny.

"Most anyone would talk to you, little boy," said Jim with a smile. "Dave won't come out again, so we might as well go back."

Rita led the way back, and Henry put Benny right in front of him where he could watch him all the way.

As they walked along, Jim said, "You people might as well stay overnight. You can cook your own trout."

"I think we must stay," said Alice. "Violet needs a good night's sleep after that scare. We all do."

At the village again, they stopped to say good-by to Rita. Henry put some money into her hand. "We'll see you again about the basket, Rita," he said. "We were all upset about Benny."

"I understand," said Rita with a smile. "I wouldn't like to lose Benny myself."

When they reached the little house, Jim said, "You can stay here as long as you want. Walk right in. If you want anything, come over and ask me. Maybe I'll have it." With that, he left them to go into the house alone.

They went up the front steps. Henry pushed open the door and they all went in. They found a small room with a fireplace. There were a few chairs and some folding cots leaning against the wall. There was one big chest of drawers.

Alice and Jessie soon found the next room which was a bedroom. Then they found the kitchen.

"There isn't any upstairs," called Benny. "Just downstairs."

"Oh, Violet!" cried Jessie. "Do look at this

dear little kitchen stove! I wish we could get our own supper."

"Jim said that campers do keep house here," said Alice. "And think of Benny's big trout. It would be fun to cook it ourselves."

"Doesn't this make you think of keeping house on Surprise Island?" cried Henry. "We'll need wood for the stove and some potatoes to go with our fish. I'll go over and ask Jim to sell us some."

"I will go with you," said Benny.

"Right," said Henry, "so you won't get out of my sight."

"I really didn't mean to," said Benny. "I was coming right back. I wanted to surprise you and find the hermit first. He said I ought to go right back, and he would take me himself. He likes to live alone."

Joe began to set up the cots. "How's this, Violet?" he said. "You three girls take the bedroom. I'll put three cots up for you. Then we three men will sleep in the living room."

"That's wonderful, Joe," said Violet. "But

let's make our own beds with our blanket rolls. We love to make beds."

"Well, I don't," said Joe. "I'll certainly let you make mine. I'll just set up the cots."

The afternoon was passing quickly away. Benny soon came back with the fish and potatoes. Henry carried a big basket of wood. "Nice, dry wood," he laughed.

Benny said, "I never thought I would just *love* dry wood."

Then they went out again to the canoes and brought up the packs. Soon Jessie and Alice had a fine fire going in the stove, while Violet got the potatoes ready.

"I think we'll eat in the kitchen," said Henry looking around. He pulled the table into the middle of the room. "Benny, see if you can find six chairs."

Violet found some heavy white plates, and set the table. Jessie cut the fish into six pieces before she cooked it. Then she put it in a big pan. For the first time in many days, they all sat down on real chairs to eat a meal at their own table. When

they had finished supper there was no food left at all.

Before long the dishes were washed, the beds were made, and everything was ready for the night. But it was not yet dark.

"Let's go out and sit on the front steps," said Jessie. "We don't want to go to bed yet."

The family went through the little house and sat down on the wooden steps. A soft wind was blowing through the trees. Soon a toad hopped out from under the steps.

"He lives there," said Benny. "I like to have toads living under our steps."

"They come out at night," said Joe. "They catch bugs."

"You know, I feel as if something will happen soon," said Violet slowly.

Alice turned to look at her. "That's funny, Violet," she said. "I feel as if we had done this before. Almost as if we had a clue and didn't know it."

Joe surprised them all by saying, "I feel that way, too."

CHAPTER 13

# The Tin Box Again

The next day the children were up early. They had breakfast. They made their beds.

"We ought to go down to see Rita the first thing we do," said Violet. "We were not very polite to her yesterday. All we could think of was Benny."

"Very well," said Alice laughing. She sat down at the kitchen table. "You four go to Rita's and Joe and I will write a letter to your grandfather."

So the four children went down the road. Rita came out when she saw them coming. She began at once to show Violet what to do next on the basket. "This will be just a small basket," she said. "You can make them as big as you want to."

When Violet finished her basket, Benny said, "That's very pretty, Violet. You can give it to Grandfather."

"So I can," said Violet, very much pleased. "He likes things we make. Now we must pay for it, Henry."

"You have paid for it already," said Rita, smiling. "The big boy paid me for the basket and the lesson and the trip into the woods. He really paid me too much." She looked at Benny and took hold of his hands. "Don't you run away, again, little boy. You make too much trouble for the hermit."

"For the *hermit!*" cried Jessie. "It was more trouble for us."

"No," said Rita, shaking her head. "Dave Hunter was upset. I could see he liked Benny. It is the first time he has said more than one word

at a time. My father says he was a very nice young man once. He built that house you are staying in."

"He did!" cried Henry. "Did he live there himself?"

"Oh, yes. Many years ago. My father told me about it last night, after you found the little boy. He said Dave went away to work, and stayed a long, long time. When he came back he was different. He stayed in his little house for about a week, and one night some mean-looking men came to see him. They had a fight, and then they went away and left Dave alone. In a few days Dave went into the woods and built his cabin and he has stayed there ever since. He wouldn't ever talk."

As the excited children started back to Old Village, Benny said, "Jessie, Jessie, maybe Dave Hunter is Bill."

"Why do you say that, young fellow?" asked Henry.

"Well, Bill could build houses. He built the little yellow house on Surprise Island and he built the little house here in Old Village."

"Maybe you're right, Benny," said Jessie in excitement. "What would we ever do without you? Let's see what Joe and Alice think."

Joe and Alice had finished their letter when the children rushed in and began to tell their story.

"So Dave Hunter built this house, did he?" said Joe. "That must have been a long time ago, for it's an old house."

"Joe, Joe! I have an idea," cried Henry. "Look around you at this house. Now—all of you pretend for a minute you're in the little yellow house on Surprise Island." He pointed around him as he went on, "There's the fireplace of the little yellow house, and there's the door, and there's the window."

"Of course," said Violet, "there's the bedroom."

"And there's the kitchen," yelled Benny. "I guess Bill could just build one kind of house."

"Why, this old house is *exactly* the same as the little yellow house!" cried Jessie; "the same front door with two windows on one side and one on the other."

"The same chimney!" shouted Benny.

"And the same front steps," said Alice slowly. "Last night I felt as if I were sitting on the steps of the little yellow house."

"So that's what it was!" cried Joe. "I felt that way, too. We sat there so many times after supper on our wedding trip."

They all looked at each other.

"Now, let's see how this was," Henry said, excitedly. "Bill lived here first. Then he went to work for Great-grandfather Alden. Then he married Mrs. McGregor, and they lived on Surprise Island where he took care of the horses."

"They lived in the little yellow house," said Benny.

"That's right," said Henry. "He built it, Grandfather said, with the help of his brother."

"Oh, that brother, Sam!" cried Joe. "He was not much good. I think Sam is the clue to this mystery."

"So do I," said Henry. "Remember Bill sold two race horses and went away without giving Mr. Alden the money."

"Now we're getting somewhere," said Joe. "That's why Bill disappeared."

"But why didn't he let his wife know where he was all those years?" asked Violet gently. "He loved Margaret."

"I don't know," said Henry. "That's the mystery. Maybe his brother wouldn't give the money back, and Bill wouldn't go home without it."

Then Violet said softly, "Joe!"

"What is it?" asked Joe quickly.

"Do you suppose Bill's brother hid the money in this house?"

"Maybe," said Joe, thinking. "But it's not a yellow house."

"Of course he did!" said Benny. "That's why Bill took the rowboat that night and came up here. I bet those mean-looking men were the friends, and they were looking for the money, too. Remember Rita said they had a fight?"

"Good, Benny," said Joe. "I guess they tried to make Bill give them the money, and Bill couldn't find it himself."

"And there's the mystery all solved," said Alice laughing.

"Well," said Henry, "I'm sure now that Dave Hunter is Bill. But where's the money, and where's the tin box?"

"Let's hunt," said Benny. "How about the chimney?"

"Not the chimney," said Henry. "Bill would have found the money if it were in the chimney."

"That's right," Benny answered.

"Not much to see," said Jessie. "A chest and a few chairs. And our cots."

"Do you think we ought to talk with the hermit, Joe?" asked Henry.

"No, not yet," answered Joe. "I don't think he would talk."

"Well, I'm not going to sit here," said Benny. "Let's do *something*."

"O.K." said Henry, getting up. "We can hunt for clues in the chest. There might be a secret drawer in it."

"Let me see," began Jessie. "The chest has

three drawers. Joe and Alice can look in one drawer, Henry and Benny in another, and Violet and I in the third."

Soon the whole family was busy. First they took the old dusty papers out of the drawers. They tapped each drawer, hunting for a secret drawer. They found nothing but dust.

"Ho-hum," said Benny. "What shall we do now, Jessie?"

"Oh, I'm sure I don't *know*," cried Jessie. Everyone looked at her.

"You're not cross, are you, Jessie?" asked Benny.

Jessie laughed a little. "Maybe I am," she said. "I did hope we would find the money in that chest. But we tapped every drawer. There is no secret drawer there. Let's go outdoors and sit on the steps."

The family went outdoors slowly and sat down on the steps. Nobody said a word. Jessie was not often cross.

Pretty soon Benny said, "I wonder where the toad is? I suppose he stays under the steps."

Alice smiled at Benny, but nobody felt like answering him.

Benny went on. "Does a toad have a house? What kind of a house does he live in, Jessie?"

"Oh, Benny! I don't *know!* I'm so tired! You want to know everything! Why do you want to ask about toads now, when we want to find a tin box!" She almost laughed.

"Never mind, Jessie," said Benny quickly. "I'll look for myself."

The little boy got down on his hands and knees. Soon he was lying on the ground looking under the steps with one eye.

"I can see him. He's just sitting there. He winked at me."

Benny picked up a long stick.

"Don't hurt the toad, Benny," said Joe.

"Oh, no. I'm just going to see how big his room is." Benny began to move the stick from one side to the other. Then he crawled quietly to the back of the steps where there was a big hole under the house. The toad jumped through the hole, and Benny followed him. Everyone

had to smile. They knew that Benny was crawling under the house.

Soon they heard him talking to himself. "Here's a pretty white stone," he was saying, "and here's an old tin can. Here's a screwdriver. Not a bad screwdriver."

Then he was silent.

But the others could hear him crawling around under the house.

"Never mind, Jessie," said Joe with a smile. "He's having fun. Children forget things very soon, you know."

Then they heard Benny say, "Well, here's the toad! Hello, Toad! Where do you live?"

"He seems to be having quite a talk with a toad," said Henry, laughing.

Benny went on, "Do you live in that old wooden box under the house? That's funny. It's open in the back instead of the front. Do you go in the back door? Why do you do that? Well, well. Ho-hum—HENRY! There's a tin box here!"

"What?" shouted Henry, almost falling down the steps.

"I've found it!" yelled Benny. "A tin box sitting right in a wooden box!"

The whole family was down on the grass looking under the steps.

"You come out, Benny!" shouted Joe. "Bring the box. We can see better out here."

"I was coming, anyway," said Benny. He came crawling as fast as he could through the hole. He pushed the tin box ahead of him, and came out from under the steps.

"Sure enough!" cried Jessie. "It *is* a tin box. I can hardly believe it. Now I only hope there is something in it."

"There is," said Benny. "I shook it."

The excited children sat back and looked at the box. "You open it, Henry," said Benny. "It's too hard for me."

Henry's hands shook as he pulled the box open. There before their eyes were piles of green bills.

"Dollar bills!" Benny whispered.

"No, Benny, they are one-hundred dollar bills!" said Henry. "I never saw one before."

"Let's count them," cried Benny.

"You count, Benny. You found them," said Jessie in a kind voice.

Benny was so excited he could hardly count straight. At last he said, "That's forty, and that's all. How much is forty one-hundred dollar bills, Henry?"

"Four thousand dollars, young fellow," said Henry. "Isn't that what two race horses would be worth, Joe?"

"Just about," said Joe.

"Boy, oh boy!" cried Benny. He was all tired out with excitement.

They all looked at each other. Then they looked at the tin box and the pile of green bills.

"Well, Joe," said Henry at last, "where do we go from here?"

"I think," answered Joe, "that when we get rested, we'd better go and see the hermit."

"The hermit is Dave Hunter. And Dave Hunter is Bill," said Benny.

"I think so, too," said Joe with a smile. "But even now, maybe he won't talk."

Jessie put her arm around her little brother.

"I'm awfully sorry I was cross, Benny," she said. "It's lucky you do want to know everything. If you hadn't looked in the toad's house, we would never have found the tin box."

CHAPTER 14

# The Hermit

Right away, the children wanted to go to see Rita again. Leaving the money in the tin box in the kitchen cupboard, the whole family almost ran up the road.

"We want to go into the woods again, Rita," Jessie called. "We want to talk with Dave Hunter. Do you think we could find our way alone?"

"Of course you can," said Rita. "But Dave won't talk."

"Maybe he will talk to Benny," said Jessie.

"Well, maybe," said Rita. "He did before."

The family started down the path through the woods. When they came to the cabin, they saw the hermit walking towards his house with a pail of water. He stopped when he saw the visitors. Then he went right on again.

"Dave!" called Henry kindly. But the hermit started to go up the steps to his cabin.

Then Benny called out in his loudest voice, "*Bill!*"

The pail went rolling down the steps as the old man stopped. He sat down and put his head in his hands.

But Benny seemed to know just what to do, and nobody stopped him. He ran over and sat down beside the old man and put his hand on his arm. "Oh, Bill," he said, "don't worry. We've come to take you home."

"Home?" said Bill. He lifted his head and looked at Benny. "I can never go home, little boy." He looked at the others as they waited on the path.

"Oh, yes, you can, Bill," cried Benny. "Grandfather wants you to come home, and so does Mrs. McGregor."

"Mrs. McGregor!" said Bill in a whisper.

Then nobody could believe what happened

next. Violet went quickly over to the steps and took the old man's hand. "He means Margaret," she said.

He looked down at the pretty little girl. "Margaret is dead," said Bill.

"No, Margaret is alive," said Violet.

"They told me she was dead," said Bill. "They said there was a fire, and the barn burned and Margaret died trying to save the horses."

"Oh, that isn't true at all, Bill," cried Benny. "We lived in that barn all last summer, and Mrs. McGregor is the housekeeper at my grandfather's house."

"I can't go home," said Bill quietly. "I can't find the money. I took Mr. Alden's money."

"We found the money," said Violet gently.

"Where?" asked the old man.

"In a tin box under the steps of the house," answered Violet.

"In a tin box—that's right," Bill said. "Oh dear, oh dear!"

Then Joe came up to the steps. He said, "Mr. McGregor, everything will be all right again, believe me. Your wife is alive and wants to see you. We just found the money today." Then he turned to the children.

"I'm afraid Bill is getting very tired," he said to them. "He is having too much excitement after forty years. Do you think you can walk to Old Village, Mr. McGregor?"

The old man looked at Joe's kind face. "Yes, I can, if all this story is true."

"I promise you it is," said Joe. Then he said to the children, "Don't ask him anything more until we get him home. But he is Bill all right."

Benny would not let go of Bill's hand. He led him carefully along the path, stopping to show him every stone.

"I've seen every stone on this path for many years, little boy," said Bill. But they all knew that he liked to have Benny help him.

They took him to the little house that he had built himself. Alice made him lie down on one of the cots, and Jessie put something soft under his head. Joe rushed over to Jim's Place and soon came back with a cup of hot tea.

"Drink this," he said. "It will make you feel better."

Bill drank the tea, and before anyone knew it, he had fallen asleep.

"He is tired out," said Violet in a whisper. "And so thin. He looks as if he didn't have enough to eat. Almost starving."

"We'll soon fix that," whispered Jessie with a smile. "He'll have enough to eat if he lives with us."

The family went into the kitchen. They shut the door softly.

"Won't Grandfather be surprised," said Henry.

"And Mrs. McGregor," said Violet.

"I'm surprised myself," said Joe. "I thought Bill was dead, for sure."

Jessie said, "Wasn't it queer how Benny got him to talk all of a sudden? Just because he called him Bill."

"Bill must have felt funny to be talking after forty years," said Benny. "I couldn't stop talking for forty years."

"I hope you won't, Benny," laughed Alice. "We love to hear you talk."

"When Bill wakes up, we must give him something to eat," said Jessie. "I think I'll run over to Jim's Place and see what he has."

"Let me go with you," said Alice. "We can go out the back door."

The two girls went across the road, and found Jim in his kitchen stirring something on the back of his stove. It was soup, and it smelled delicious.

Jim turned around quickly and asked, "Wasn't that the hermit I saw with you?"

"Yes, it was," said Jessie. "His real name is Bill McGregor, and he used to work for our great-grandfather."

"I thought something was queer about him," cried Jim. "People used to say that little house was Bill McGregor's place. Then one day Dave Hunter came to Old Village and said it was his. He said he was a cousin of Bill's.

"But he wouldn't live in the house. He told me to use it for campers and he built himself his cabin."

"Well," said Alice, "he says he is Bill McGregor now."

"He talks, does he?" asked Jim. "I can hardly believe it. It must seem strange. He's a nice, gentle old man. I always was sorry for him. I always tried to feed him up when he came out of the woods."

"That's what we came for," said Jessie. "Something to feed to him. That hot soup would be just the thing."

"Jes-*sie!*" Benny called from across the road. "Bill's awake and he's hungry."

"Take some bread and butter, too," said Jim with a laugh. "That'll do him good."

Alice and Jessie hurried back. Bill was sitting up in a chair. He looked rested.

Jessie put a little table in front of him, and set down the hot soup and a plate of bread and butter. Bill ate as if he were half-starved.

"You don't look as thin as you did, Bill," said Benny. "A little fatter."

Everyone laughed, even Bill himself. "I don't think he grew very fat on one bowl of soup," said Jessie. "But you do look better, Bill, sure enough."

"I feel better," said the old man, looking into

the girl's kind face. Then he looked around at the other friendly faces. They were all smiling at him.

"I suppose Mrs. McGregor won't know you," said Benny.

"I will know her," said Bill, "even if she is old."

"She might like you better without your long beard," said Benny.

"Sh-sh, Benny," said Jessie.

But Bill's feelings were not hurt. He even laughed a little. "My beard can be cut off," he said. "Then I will look like Bill McGregor instead of an old hermit."

"Jessie!" said Benny, all of a sudden. "Where did you get that soup? I'm awfully hungry."

"What do you know!" cried Henry. "It's long past noon and we were so excited we forgot our own dinner."

"Don't worry," said Jessie, getting up at once. "We'll soon fix that."

CHAPTER 15

# Starting for Home

The family sat down on the steps the next morning after breakfast.

"I want to go home," said Benny suddenly.

"We all want to go home," said Henry. "But how can we? We can't take Bill in a canoe. Four people are too many."

"We'll have to get to Mr. Long's store some way," said Jessie. "If only we had our station wagon."

"Let's wait a little while," said Joe. "Maybe something will happen." He winked at Alice.

Benny rushed over to Joe and shook his shoulder. "What are you winking at Alice for?" he cried.

"Don't you wish you knew?" teased Joe. He rolled Benny over in the grass.

"Get up and look what's coming, boys," called Alice. She pointed up the road. Coming around the corner was their very own station wagon.

"It's the station wagon!" shouted Benny. "That's Mr. Long driving and his boy is with him." Benny began to jump up and down. He waved with both hands.

Mr. Long soon saw him, stopped at the little house, and got out. He laughed to see the children so surprised.

"You didn't hear us, did you?" he said. "Joe and I made a lot of plans up at my store that first day."

"Henry, I was sure you heard us," said Joe, laughing. "I had just asked Mr. Long to meet us here in six days, when you suddenly came around the corner."

"No, I didn't hear a word," said Henry, smiling. "But Mr. Long came on the right day. We do want to go home."

"I never thought I would want this trip to end," said Violet. "But now I want to get home to see Grandfather, and we all want to get Bill home to Mrs. McGregor."

"Don't tell me you have found Bill!" said Mr. Long, much surprised.

"Oh, yes," said Benny. "Remember Dave Hunter, the hermit?"

"Yes," said Mr. Long, "you mean he is Bill?"

Jessie said, "Yes, and it's going to be a big surprise for Mrs. McGregor. Joe, shouldn't we send a telegram to Grandfather?"

"Good for you, Jessie," said Joe. "We'll do that, just as soon as we find a place."

"Come on," shouted Benny. "Let's go."

The little house was soon full of people rushing around, rolling up bed rolls. They put things into the back of the station wagon, while Jim packed a big lunch for them to eat on the way home.

Jessie took the money out of the tin box and put it carefully into her handbag. "I'll take care of this," she said.

"We carry that money around as if it were just pieces of old paper," said Violet laughing.

"It is," said Benny, as he carried his bed roll to the station wagon.

"Why not let me cut off that long beard, before you go, Mr. McGregor?" asked Jim, when he came over with the lunch. "I can cut it for you."

"How do you feel about it, Bill?" asked Joe. "Do you want it off?"

"Of course I do," said Bill. "Don't you remember I said I would look more like Bill McGregor?"

So the family all watched Jim as he cut off Bill's long beard, then shaved him.

"What a change!" said Joe. "You certainly look fine, Bill."

"A fine-looking man," said Jim. "Look at yourself, Mr. McGregor."

"Yes, you've got a nice smooth face," said Benny. "Mrs. McGregor will like you better this way."

"Oh, dear," said Jessie suddenly, "we forgot all about the two canoes. We can't leave them here."

"Yes, you can," said Mr. Long. "That's why I brought my boy with me. We can paddle them back. Don't worry about the canoes or the tents. We'll take them with us."

Benny took Bill's hand, and said, "You'll be surprised, Bill, when you see where Mrs. McGregor lives. Grandfather's big house is very nice."

Bill smiled at the little boy. "I know that house very well," he said.

"What are you going to do about this house, Dave—Bill, I mean?" asked Jim Carr. "And your cabin in the woods?"

"You can have them both," said Bill quietly. "You were always very kind to me, and gave me things to eat when I didn't even say thank you."

"That's all right," said Jim. "And thank *you.*

Nobody ever gave me two houses in one day."

At last everything was ready. Bill sat in front with Benny and Joe who was going to drive. Alice and Violet sat behind them. Henry and Jessie sat on the back seat.

"Now we're really going home!" shouted Benny. "We did find Bill and we did find the money, Joe. Won't Grandfather be glad!"

Joe turned the station wagon around, and the children waved good-by until they were out of sight of Old Village.

"Little boy," said Bill suddenly, "how much money was in that tin box?"

"It was all hundred-dollar bills," said Benny. "And it was four thousand dollars in all."

"Four thousand dollars," said Bill in great excitement. "That's exactly right. Who did you say put it there?"

"We aren't sure," said Joe, kindly. "You must tell us that."

"I'm afraid it was my own brother, Sam," Bill told them sadly. "I understand the whole thing now."

"Tell us," begged Jessie. "Tell us everything you know."

"Well," began Bill in a weak voice, "did you hear about the horses? I sold two fine race horses for Mr. Alden."

"He was not our grandfather," said Jessie. "That Mr. Alden is dead."

"Oh, dear. I suppose so," said Bill. "He is Mr. Alden to me, because I worked for him. Your grandfather is James Alden. Well, my brother Sam told me to give him the money, and he could make three times as much. So I gave it to him."

"That was when you lived on the island," said Henry.

"Yes, he told me not to say a word, but to come to Maine and soon I could come home with a lot of money to pay Mr. Alden."

"And what did you do next?" asked Alice.

"I came up here to meet my brother," said Bill. "And then I heard he was killed by a car. I hunted all over my house for a tin box. But I never could find it. His friends didn't know where it was. So I shut up my little yellow house, and went to live in the woods."

"Yellow? You mean your yellow house on Surprise Island?" asked Henry, wondering.

"No, I mean my yellow house right here in Old Village."

"But the house we were in is brown, Bill," Jessie told him kindly.

"Well, yes, my dear," said Bill, almost whispering. "It is brown now. But it used to be yellow. It has been painted since then."

CHAPTER 16

# A Happy Home

The family had not gone very far when suddenly Joe stopped the car by the side of the road.

"What's the matter?" asked Henry.

"Bill's getting too tired," answered Joe quietly. "This is all too much of a change for him. I'm going to fix a bed on the back seat so he can lie down."

Benny looked up at Bill and saw that it was true. The old man was very white, and his hands were shaking.

"Oh, dear," said Jessie. "We talked to him too much. He isn't used to it."

She and Alice helped Joe make a soft bed of

blankets on the back seat. Bill did not say a word. Joe and Henry took his arms and helped him out of the front seat and into the back. Bill lay down at once and shut his eyes, as if he were very glad to lie down.

The three girls took the middle seat and Henry got up in front beside Benny.

"He'll be all right," said Joe, looking back at Bill. "You can talk all you want to. I think he'll sleep."

"Let's send that telegram to Grandfather at the next village," said Jessie. "What shall we say?"

"Ten words," said Benny.

"No, you can send fifteen," said Henry. "Let's make up a telegram as we ride. We should certainly begin, 'Found Bill and the money.' "

"Five words," said Violet, counting.

" 'All coming home today,' " said Jessie. "That's four more. Nine so far."

"Then we can have six more words," said Benny. "We ought to say, 'We may be late for supper.' "

"We certainly will be late for supper," said Joe.

Then Alice said, "Benny, don't you think we should say something about Bill, like 'Weak and tired'? Then Mrs. McGregor won't expect the big strong man who used to lift the boat."

Benny counted on his fingers for a few minutes. Then he cried, "We can say it this way. 'Found Bill and money. Bill very weak. All coming home today late for supper. Hello.' "

"Wonderful, Benny!" said Joe, laughing. "Your grandfather will know you made up that telegram for sure. I always like to say hello at the end of a telegram!"

Henry said, "Now Benny, don't forget what you said. Keep saying it over and over until we come to a village."

This gave Benny something to do. When they did stop at a village he could remember every word.

As the girl wrote down the telegram, Jessie cried, "Henry, let's say it's from the Boxcar Children!"

The girl stopped writing, and looked up in surprise. "Are *you* the four children who lived in a boxcar?" she asked.

"Yes, we did," said Benny. "We had fun."

"And you found your grandfather at last," she cried. She looked from one smiling face to another. "I read about you in the paper. But I never expected to see you."

"This telegram is to our grandfather," said Benny. "And you can say it's from the Boxcar Children, and Alice and Joe. He'll know."

"Yes, I guess he will," laughed the girl. "I'll send it right off. It will get to him in an hour."

"Fine," said Henry, paying for the telegram. "Now let's get on our way."

Bill was still asleep when they got into the station wagon again. He was still asleep at lunch time. They did not wake him for lunch.

"He needs sleep more than food now," said Joe.

"I do hope he isn't sick," said Alice in a worried voice.

"I don't think he is," said Joe. "I think he's

had just too much excitement. It is such a change from not talking at all."

"It shows us we'll have to be very careful of Bill," said Jessie. "But I can hardly wait to ask him the end of that story."

Bill slept almost all the afternoon. As they came near home, they had to wake him up. When they drove up to the door of their grandfather's house, Bill was sitting up very straight.

Mr. Alden was sitting on the porch in a big chair. Beside him was Mrs. McGregor. They were waiting.

Bill leaned forward to look. "It's my Margaret!" he said, almost crying. "She has the same beautiful blue eyes!"

Joe and Henry helped the old man out of the car and up the steps.

"Bill!" cried Margaret. She put both arms around him and led him to her chair. "It's all right, Bill! It's all right!" she said, over and over.

Just then there was a very loud noise from upstairs. It seemed to come from Jessie's room. It was Watch. He came rushing down the stairs and out of the door, barking and barking. He could not believe that his four children had come back to him again. At last he lay down by Jessie's feet, tired out.

"Now I guess he will eat his meals," said Mr. Alden. "As for Mrs. McGregor, she hasn't eaten a good meal since you all went away."

Benny said, "I think it's funny. We have so many people that can't eat. I don't have any trouble eating *my* meals."

"Now that we're all together again, Benny," said Grandfather laughing, "everyone will be all right. I think I shall eat better myself. We have things for supper that you like best. There is hamburger for you. Bill always liked fish best and that's what he'll have. There's ham for Joe and apple pie for Jessie."

"No pie for me?" asked Benny, taking his grandfather's hand.

"What do you think?" teased his grandfather. "I don't believe anyone will go hungry tonight."

It was wonderful to see Bill eat. With his Margaret beside him again, he seemed like a different man.

"I feel better and better," he said.

After supper the family sat again on the porch.

"Joe," whispered Benny, "couldn't we talk to Bill now? He seems all right to me."

"You can try," said Joe. "We'll soon see how he takes it. We can stop if he gets too upset."

Benny went over then to Bill and Margaret. He put his hand over Bill's.

"We want to ask you just a few more things, Bill," he said. "Are you too tired?"

"No, little boy," said Bill. "I don't think I shall ever be tired again. Ask me anything you want."

Benny looked at Joe. Joe smiled back at him.

Then Benny said, "We want to know something more about your brother. How was he going to make the money three times as much?"

"I didn't know myself at first," answered Bill. "But later I found out he was going to give it to some friends of his to bet on the horse races."

"Oh, but he might have lost it all!" cried Henry.

"Yes, I know that now," said Bill. "His friends were bad people, I'm afraid. Sam would have been all right if his friends had let him alone. But he always did what they said, and I always did what my brother Sam said."

He looked around sadly. "One night after Sam was killed, these men came up to Maine. They hunted all over my house, but they couldn't find the money. I didn't know where the tin box was myself. But they didn't believe me. They tried to make me tell, and we had a great fight. But at last they went away, and I never saw them again."

"Were they the ones who told you the barn was burned?" asked Mr. Alden.

"Yes. They didn't want me to go home and tell all I knew, so they told me Margaret was dead."

"I suppose that finished you," said Benny.

Bill smiled at him. "Yes, that finished me. I didn't want to live any more without Margaret, and I didn't want to see people. Besides, I couldn't come home without the money, so I went into the deep woods to live alone forever."

"Oh, I'm so glad we found you!" said Jessie

suddenly. "Supposing we had never asked to go into the little yellow house on Surprise Island! Now you and Mrs. McGregor can live right here in her rooms, can't they, Grandfather?"

"If her rooms are big enough," said Mr. Alden.

"Three rooms ought to be big enough for two people," said Mrs. McGregor, happily.

"I can help with the horses," said Bill. "Do you still have horses?"

"Yes, we have two," answered Mr. Alden. "But you will rest a long time before doing any work."

Darkness began to fall. The birds began to sing their evening songs. The family sat quietly for a minute and listened.

Then Violet said, "Isn't this a happy house, Alice? You and Joe so happy on the top floor—"

"And Bill and Mrs. McGregor will be in their own little rooms," cried Benny.

"Don't forget us," said Henry, "with our mystery all solved, and getting back to Grandfather."

"And we'll all go and live in the little yellow house on Surprise Island every summer," said Benny.

"Hold on, my boy. Not so fast!" said Mr. Alden. "That's Bill's house."

"Oh, so it is," said Benny. "Well then, he and Mrs. McGregor can live in it every summer, and we can go over to see them."

"Well, we'll see," said Mr. Alden with a smile.

Violet suddenly put her hand on her grandfather's knee, and looked up into his kind face. She could not see very well, for it had grown quite dark. But she knew he was smiling at her.

"Grandfather," she asked, "couldn't you use some of that money to fix up the little yellow house on Surprise Island? It is so dusty and the chairs are so old."

"A fine idea!" said Mr. Alden, taking her small hand in his big one. "We could buy a lot of chairs with that money. And by the way, where *is* the money?"

"Right here!" said Jessie at once. She took it

out of her handbag and gave it to Mr. Alden.

"Maybe Bill and I could paper and paint the rooms before school begins," said Henry.

"Oh, we could all paint!" shouted Benny, jumping around. "Let's paint the outside, too."

"That would be fun," said Alice. "Joe and I could help you every day after work on the cave."

"Right now you children have something new to think about," said Joe. "We will take a lunch over every day, and work until we get the house all fixed up."

Violet sat down beside her grandfather in his great chair. He moved over quickly to make room for her and put his arm around her.

"I'm glad the little yellow house isn't a sad place to you any more, Grandfather," she said, leaning her head back against his arm. "It's going to be a happy place again.."

"We'll still paint it yellow," said Benny. "Ho-hum!"

"What does 'ho-hum' mean this time, Ben?" asked Henry, laughing at his little brother.

Mrs. McGregor answered, smiling at Bill, "To me it means, 'Thank you, children.' "

Mr. Alden said, "To me it means I'm very glad you are all at home again."

"Well," said Benny, "what I really mean is that I can hardly wait until tomorrow to paint that little yellow house!"

GERTRUDE CHANDLER WARNER discovered when she was teaching that many readers who like an exciting story could find no books that were both easy and fun to read. She decided to try to meet this need, and her first book, *The Boxcar Children*, quickly proved she had succeeded.

Miss Warner drew on her own experiences to write the mystery. As a child she spent hours watching trains go by on the tracks opposite her family home. She often dreamed about what it would be like to set up housekeeping in a caboose or freight car—the situation the Alden children find themselves in.

When Miss Warner received requests for more adventures involving Henry, Jessie, Violet, and Benny Alden, she began additional stories. In each, she chose a special setting and introduced unusual or eccentric characters who liked the unpredictable.

While the mystery element is central to each of Miss Warner's books, she never thought of them as strictly juvenile mysteries. She liked to stress the Aldens' independence and resourcefulness and their solid New England devotion to using up and making do. The Aldens go about most of their adventures with as little adult supervision as possible—something else that delights young readers.

Miss Warner lived in Putnam, Connecticut, until her death in 1979. During her lifetime, she received hundreds of letters from girls and boys telling her how much they liked her books. And so she continued the Aldens' adventures, writing a total of nineteen books in the Boxcar Children series.